Frank Ronan

THE BETTER ANGEL

sceptre

Copyright © 1992 by Frank Ronan

First published in Great Britain in 1992 by Bloomsbury Publishing Ltd

Sceptre edition 1993

Sceptre is an imprint of Hodder and Stoughton Paperbacks, a division of Hodder and Stoughton Ltd

Printed and bound in Great Britain for Hodder and Stoughton Paperbacks, a division of Hodder and Stoughton Ltd., Mill Road, Dunton Green, Sevenoaks, Kent TN13 2YA. (Editorial Office: 47 Bedford Square, London WC1B 3DP) by Clays Ltd., St Ives plc.

A C.I.P. catalogue for this title is available from the British Library

ISBN 0-340-58124-7

THE FIRST YEAR

SEPTEMBER

The day I first met Smallgods Temple I woke to the sound of my father breathing in his sleep. I thought I must have been mistaken because normally he was up before me and away working the fields by the time I was conscious. Sometimes I would be aware of his lips brushing against my eyebrow just before he left the bedroom, and the rattle of plumbing behind the walls, but only just aware of it; the stir my father made in waking was insinuated into my dreams.

That morning I descended slowly from the heights of sleep to find that he was still there. His huge right hand, bigger than my entire face, was prone on the pillow like a child's hand, and his nostrils were quivering with the stale breath of sleep. I thought that I might have woken too early, out of nervousness, because it was the first day back to school after the holidays, but when a breeze from the open window stirred the curtains I could see that the sun was already well risen, and the chill of the morning was giving way to summer heat. 'Dad,' I said. 'Dad?'

I put my feet out on to the linoleum and pulled my pyjama bottoms about to cover the morning indecency. Like him I slept bare-chested for the summer, with two pillows for each of us, and a glass of milk on the table between in case either should wake thirsty in the night. I crossed to his bed and put my hand to his shoulder. 'Dad?'

As he began to wake, his face broke into a smile. 'John G.,' he said.

'It's late, Dad.'

'I know.'

While I went to pull the curtains open I could hear his fingernails rasping in his chest hair. 'Well, *a ghrá*,' he said, 'there has to be a first time for everything.'

The two words of love in Gaelic were part of our private life. My father used them in that bedroom and nowhere else, and I had never heard him use them to my older brother Gerard or my aunt Dervla.

I said nothing, but leaned out of the window to see what the day would be like, and also to give him a chance to get out of bed unobserved. There was the rustle of bedclothes and the slight odour of male flesh as he passed behind me, taking his clothes to the bathroom with him to dress. Then, while I waited my turn, there was the smell of ripening apples in the garden, and the steady noise of a gang of chickens working over the haggard.

Over the sixteen years I had been sleeping with him things had become a little more complicated. To begin with I had been pressed against him in the big double bed, with my thumb in my mouth and my face smothered in fur. From time to time Dervla would raise objections to that arrangement, and say it wasn't natural, and that I was getting too big. When I was about eleven my father agreed with her and I was put into a room of my own, where I roared with nightmares for a month and wet the bed twice. It took a major conspiracy between my father and myself to hide the first wetting from Dervla, and when it happened the second time he said nothing, but threw the double bed out of his room and installed two small ones instead, and I returned, not held to his breast as I had been in my childhood, but near enough still to know when he turned in his sleep and to turn in sympathy.

In all those years I never saw my father naked; but once, by accident, when I was fourteen or so, the outline of a morning erection became apparent in his pyjama bottoms. I don't know if I had been aware of the existence of that phenomenon in him before, but afterwards I avoided looking in his direction whenever there was a possibility of seeing it again. If I ejaculated in my sleep, I would wake up directly afterwards, paralysed with self-consciousness, wondering if he noticed the smell, or whether I had been making a noise. I didn't want all that. Things were easier when I was ten, and we were like two children in the same bed.

He returned from the bathroom, washed and shaved, while I was still leaning out of the window. 'You'd better hurry, *a ghrá*,' he said. 'It's late.'

'I know,' I said.

I went to the bathroom, where clean underpants and socks and a shirt were laid out, freshly ironed, and a clean pair of jeans with sharp creases was hanging over the back of the chair. I borrowed my father's razor to deal with the ratty shadow on my upper lip, and while I was about it examined my skin for signs of adolescent eruption. I was not given to spots, thank God, but vigilance was necessary, just in case.

My father was still in the bedroom when I had finished. He was sitting on the low windowsill with the sun at his back, and his hands hanging awkwardly between his knees. There was something about him that disturbed me, only for a second. There was something less pink in his complexion; something more hollow in the flesh that fell from his cheekbones; something rounded in his shoulders. The man who had always made me feel small looked small himself.

Dervla was waiting in the kitchen with a cup of thick tea, the milk and sugar already stirred in. When my father entered the room just behind me she looked as though she was witnessing the raising of the dead. For once she was speechless.

My father said, 'I slept.'

He closed his hand around the back of my neck for a second before going out to the haggard to see if he could catch up on some of the work before he had to drive me to school.

Dervla, my mother's younger, unmarried sister, who had given up her university studies to be a mother to Gerard and me, pulled the chair out from in front of my breakfast plate and held on to the back of it until I sat down. The plate was heaped with fried pig in various guises, and two runny eggs. She remained behind me until I began to eat. In the meantime she said, 'I hope your father isn't getting sick. I have a terrible feeling.'

'Black pudding,' I said.

'School,' she said. 'It's a long time until your lunch.'

All of my life I had eaten black pudding as a duty, until last spring, when Dervla and I had had a running battle over it. It had disappeared from the menu for the summer, but now it was back, four thick slices set artistically at the cardinal points of the plate. I poured the ketchup while I was considering what to do, and then whistled one of the dogs in from the porch and flipped the pudding through the air and into his mouth, a piece at a time. I wouldn't look at Dervla to see what her reaction might be, but as she turned to the Rayburn to make my fried bread I heard myself say, 'There has to be a first time for everything.'

'Gerard came back last night,' she said. 'He's still in the bed.'

'He must have been late.'

'About one,' she said. 'You know Gerard.'

We saw very little of Gerard in those days. He was mostly in Dublin, cultivating a ponytail. He had dropped out of college the year before to work for a record company. He appeared from time to time and tried to corrupt me in the nicest sort of way, with proscribed drugs and satanic music; but we never really managed to get over a lifetime of loathing each other. It wasn't my fault that my father had nothing to say to him, but still, I was held responsible.

I said, 'Will he be here when I get back from school?'

'I don't know,' Dervla said. 'I didn't speak to him. All I know is that his car is in the yard, and there was a strange-looking yoke of a coat on the floor in the hall. Well, it might be a coat, but I've never seen the likes of it. Do you want plain fried bread or eggy bread?'

'I have two eggs already.'

Instead of taking that as a no, she went ahead with making eggy bread, I suppose to compensate for the black pudding, and I ate it all, for the same reason.

Because it was a schoolday, I had only the one job to do that morning. As soon as breakfast had been dealt with I went to get Oedipus in from the long field and put him in his stable for the day. We were trying to get the fat off him for the hunting in November. It wasn't my fault he was called Oedipus. It was Dervla who gave the horses those names. Oedipus got his because he was blind in one eye. Her own hunter was called Odysseus because of his tendency to wander, and she had a brood mare called Clytemnestra who had once kicked an Arab teaser to death. The next foal this mare had was to be called Electra or Orestes, depending on its sex. Dervla was living out the degree in classics she never finished at Trinity.

Oedipus was a big gaunt horse who would have been a steeplechaser if it hadn't been for his blindness. He was slow in the box and like a mad bullock after the hunt. He was bought for my father at about the time that my father stopped hunting and I grew a sudden six inches, so he became my horse. Gerard had too much of the sophisticate about him for hunting in Wexford.

The long field stretched over the headland and down to the river. There were heifers around the gate, but the horses were below the brow of the hill and out of sight, so I had to stand on the gate and shout for them. Odysseus came galloping up with his tail over his back like a carthorse and Oedipus wandered after him with his head to the ground. I rode Oedipus back without a halter, the two of us snatching blackberries from the hedges, while the other horse trotted ahead, snorting and shying. The lane was green still, even after the hot summer, overhung with oak trees and carpeted with nettles. It wasn't until we were back in the yard that I began to think about the year of school ahead of me; the last year.

I gave Oedipus his feed, and said to him, 'This is going to be the worst year of my life.'

Smallgods Temple sat between me and the window. On that first morning he had arrived in school before me and occupied the seat that was mine by rights. It was the place with the best view, out across the fields and down to the same river that flowed past my house. There were windows on the other side of the classroom, but they looked towards the town, and even if you found urban landscapes interesting, Kilnure was a dingy place, with nothing to divert you apart from dogs copulating in the streets. On coming into the classroom that morning, I had glared at the stranger who had usurped me, but he had taken no notice and I had settled for the second-best seat, one removed from the window.

He was arousing a covert interest among the others in the class. No one had heard him speak or knew his name. When Godfrey Temple was called for in the roll, and he answered to it, a snigger went around the class. It wasn't just that it was a joke name, it was also the way in which he answered. Everyone else mumbled, '*Anseo*,' when it was their turn, picking at their desks and pretending that the ceremony had nothing to do with them. But he called out, 'Here!' in a clear, abrasive voice.

The master said, 'We use the Gaelic here. *Anseo* will do.'

And Smallgods Temple said, 'I prefer not to use it, if you don't mind terribly.'

The air was swollen with suffocated laughter, and the master, who was one of the more humane of our teachers, decided to let it pass, and went on to the next name on his list. People were looking in the stranger's direction and giggling.

At that stage, no one believed that he really spoke like that. They thought he was putting it on to annoy the master.

His next opportunity to open his mouth was during our first lesson, which was English, and a poem by Stephen Sinnot was being discussed. He didn't put his hand in the air to speak like the rest of us, but cut into a gap in the discussion with his voice.

'Excuse me,' he said, 'I don't agree with that.'

'Yes?' the master said. Mr Bates was a nervous individual, destined for the priesthood and the missions, after several years of failing to deal with us.

Smallgods said, 'Stephen Sinnot had no political motive in writing that poem. It is a love poem, and the metaphors are bisexual rather than bipartisan.'

This time there were guffaws in the classroom. No one was in any doubt that he was trying to get a rise out of the master. In the middle of the laughter, Smallgods added 'sir' to the end of his sentence. It seemed like comic timing.

Poor Mr Bates was trying not to blush. He had an unfortunate habit of wagging his finger at us when he was angry. We could see his hand rise into the wagging position. But he would do his best to treat his interlocutor seriously. Part of his misfortune was that he was prepared to see some nobility in our savageness.

'Would you like to explain that?' he said.

And then Smallgods Temple rattled on for four and a half minutes, claiming insights into the poem that no one could have read from the text. Mr Bates seemed unsure whether to be pleased that there was a degree of intelligence showing in his class, or furious that he was being shown up by a schoolboy. Finally, with some exasperation, he cut into Smallgods' diatribe by saying, 'So why is the first line of the poem, "Between the green and the orange I lie"?'

Smallgods said, 'Funnily enough, I asked Stephen that the

last time I spoke to him. He said it was a device to throw the duller academics off the scent. Of course you can't believe everything Stephen says.'

All poor Mr Bates could say was, 'Well, having dealt with that, perhaps we should get back to the English class. We are only here to pass exams, you know.'

Smallgods shrugged his shoulders and turned to look out of the window. There was no more laughter in the classroom. I don't know if Smallgods was aware of it, but he had damned himself in the eyes of most people. Firstly, because it had become apparent that the voice he was using was real, and secondly because he had talked at length like an egghead, using words that most of us wouldn't choose to understand. And worst of all there was the boasting, or name-dropping, when he claimed acquaintance with a poet who most of us hadn't known was still alive. Now he kept watch out of the window, as if he agreed with the others that he shouldn't have been in that room in the first place.

He was blocking part of my view. The river was changing colour and there was a shadow crossing the hill on the other side. Mr Bates' class had ended, and he had left the room, almost without my noticing. Cochran turned around in the desk in front of us and said, 'Jesus, boys, will you look at the lads?'

It must have looked odd, both of us side by side and intent on the landscape beyond. I was only doing what I had always done: it was the stranger doing it as well that made it seem bizarre.

Someone sniggered behind us. It was probably Mulally. Smallgods Temple turned to look at me directly for the first time. He had those very pale eyes. Do you know? Those eyes that are so unsettling in strangers. The only sort of eyes you ever really notice. I tried to ignore him, and the rest of them, but I was caught out, because in looking out of the window I was also looking at Smallgods. I lifted the lid of my desk and fossicked inside for the books that were needed for the next lesson.

He said, 'Why is your nose crooked?'

'What?' I said, taking my head out of the desk.

Cochran was having a good time. 'Fuck, lads,' he squealed. 'Moore have a bent nose.'

Someone else said, 'Fucksake, Moore, you're a marked man, whah?'

I couldn't understand why the stranger had said that, unless it was because I was the only person there he hadn't offended so far. I looked at his own neat triangular nose and thought about altering it with a box. But it was only speculative. There wasn't enough anger in me to carry my fist through the air. My nose had been crooked for five years, since a horse had stood on it, but no one had noticed until now. I thought the only way to save my dignity was to answer him as though he had asked a reasonable question. But I wasn't going to admit to being stood on by a horse; not among those people.

'I was hit by a sliotar,' I said. Anyone could have told it was a lie since I had never played hurling in my life, but they wanted to believe it.

'Jesus, that must have been some smack. Whah?'

'You're not serious.'

'Fucksake and all the boys.'

That would do for them. Even the stranger was smiling.

As the heat of the morning increased, a certain atmosphere began to build up in the classroom: the heavy scent of thirty young men in late summer, not all of whom were overconcerned with hygiene. Just before the break, one of the masters had some more windows opened, but there was no great improvement. When the bell rang at a quarter past eleven there was a rush for the door, and a temporary worsening of the smell with the movement of bodies.

I took my time reaching the shop, so as to get there

after the crush, but still I had to wait while six or seven people in front of me bought single cigarettes. Coming back, I saw Smallgods Temple by the school gates, looking down his nose at a football game in the yard below him. He saw me, and there was something of a greeting in his expression.

'Did I hear your name is John Moore?' he said.

I said that it was. My name was no secret. But I wasn't sure if I wanted to talk to him. I was thinking about moving to another part of the classroom. Out of the limelight.

'From Roscarmony?' he said.

I didn't ask him how he knew it. He could have found out from anyone. 'Roscarmony,' I said.

'You used to go hunting when you were little?'

I didn't know what to say to that. I could have said that I still did. But I decided to say nothing.

'You don't remember me. When we were about six. We used to come down to stay with my grandmother and I was taken out hunting, on a leading rein. I persuaded them to take my leading rein off because you didn't have one. I used to talk to you.'

I shook my head.

He said, 'I recognised you. But it took me a while to fit it all together. Your father was an enormous man on an enormous horse. You could have ridden under its belly if you wanted. I remember you used to follow behind him and I followed you. You had a grey pony with a funny name. Was it Greek? Philip? No; something longer.'

'Philoctetes,' I said. 'He was always going lame.'

He laughed. There weren't many who would have got the joke. 'You remember,' he said.

'No,' I said. 'I have a terrible memory. I don't know how you can remember it all.'

He said, 'You haven't changed that much since you were six. Except that you were called John G. Not John.'

'I'm John now,' I said. I tried not to sound alarmed. Being called John G. in school was my nightmare. The bell was ringing, and the football game below was breaking up. People were retrieving their jumpers from the goalposts.

As I was getting into bed that night, I noticed an alarm clock on the table. My father said, 'I got the softest one I could. I hope it doesn't wake you.'

'I'd sleep through anything,' I said. I was still trying to remember the stranger out hunting when I was six. There was no image in my head that I could make to fit him.

OCTOBER

You may be confused by now, because I refer to him as Smallgods Temple. Smallgods was his name at home, and although I wasn't to hear of it for another five months, you will have to forgive me for using it here, because if I called him Godfrey, or Temple, I would have no visual idea of the man I was talking about. He acquired that name because his father was also called Godfrey, and his father tried to make him spell it with a lower-case 's' because he had such deep religious sensibilities that a capital would have been considered sacrilegious. Once Smallgods had acquired that name, his father became known to his wife and children as Oldgods, but never to his face. I am only telling you all of this now on the condition that you understand I knew none of it at the time.

What I did gather, fairly early on, was that Oldgods Temple was a poet who wrote in Gaelic, and an Englishman to boot. That they had lived on the south side of Dublin until the death of Smallgods' grandmother, when they had come to live at her house, at a place called Ballynell, which was four or five miles up the river from Roscarmony, where I lived. That they had a house in Italy, near a place called Busto Arsizio, where they spent holidays. What I didn't understand was why, if Smallgods had a background as wealthy and cultivated as it seemed, he was attending the Christian Brothers school at Kilnure.

I didn't move to another part of the classroom. Smallgods and I changed places so that I was back beside my window, and had him as a buffer zone between me and my education. From time to time he would hiss acid remarks at me so that I was choking with laughter during mathematics and German. Often a Christian Brother or a master would glare at us.

'Would you like to tell us what you find so funny, Moore?'

'Nothing, sir.'

'Well, perhaps you would like to repeat the last thing I said.'

'It was something about logarithms, sir.'

'Is that so, Moore? The trouble with you people is that you like to pretend you are grown-up. But you still don't know how to behave yourselves.'

By now he would be glaring at Smallgods, who had kept a straight face throughout, and Smallgods would smile at him. Sometimes he irritated the masters so much that they seemed as if they were on the point of hitting him. They would hand his essays back to him and say, 'Very pretty, Temple. But you won't pass an exam with that sort of waffle.'

The only teacher who was on our side was Moran, the mad art mistress. If our behaviour got out of hand and she had to lose her temper with us, she would screech, 'Oh, the two of yous should be tied together!' And she would fling back her vast tangle of hair when her tantrum had been expressed, and then smile at us, but with her eyes cast down, and so we would return to our serious study of Marcel Duchamp and the Dada Movement.

The lunches that Dervla packed for me were heavier than my books, with every slab of ham sandwich wrapped separately and a three-pint flask of strong tea. When Smallgods brought a lunch with him the sandwiches would be filled with venison or smoked salmon or pheasant. But more often than not he would have no lunch at all, and say that he had forgotten it, or that he didn't like to eat so early in the day. He would sit with me and watch me devour my mounds of food so that I felt like a barbarian to be eating at all.

Every morning, when my father dropped me at the school

gates, he would say to me, 'Have you money?' And if I said that I hadn't, he would pull a handful of notes from his pocket, and I would take a crushed pound from it, or whatever I needed. But Smallgods never seemed to have money and never went to the shop at breaktime. He stayed at the gate looking down over the football as if he thought he was Zeus on Olympus. Towards the end of October I noticed that the soles were coming away from his shoes, but at the time I thought he was too wealthy and unworldly to worry about things like that.

NOVEMBER

As the darkness of November began to gather about us, and the winter hardened the ground beneath our feet, a hardness of a different kind came into the school. It was something that had been threatening us for four years or more, but which most of us had managed to ignore.

In that last year, the prospect of the rest of our lives began to loom, and people became serious as they jostled for a head-start. We were told that those who failed the final exams failed in life, and were destined to be winos and bagmen or, if they were lucky, roadsweepers. At seventeen and eighteen we were dividing ourselves into the fatcats and the hopeless. Reality, as it was represented to us, intimidated overgrown boys into adopting the seriousness of bank clerks in their studies. Rebels and anarchists who had wept at the death of Sid Vicious were filling out civil-service application forms, and one by one, as the exams came nearer, people were lost into another world, where paying attention in the classroom was nothing to be ashamed of.

There were a few of us who retained the old dignity of slackness: the stupid, the careless and the arrogant; typified respectively by Cochran, me, and Smallgods. Between us we did what we could to alleviate the studious atmosphere. Cochran and I both had farms to fall into, and Smallgods thought he was clever enough to pass exams without studying. When I asked him what he was going to do, he said that he was going to university, and when I asked him what he was going to do there, he said that it didn't matter. He said that four years at university was a qualification to do whatever you liked. But the main thing was that we weren't racing to the foot of the management and accountancy ladders, or killing ourselves to get into medicine for the sake of respectability.

DECEMBER

It was the first Wednesday in December when Smallgods asked me why I never came to school on Tuesdays.

'Flu,' I said. There were others listening. Later, when we were alone, I told him the real reason.

'So you still hunt?' he said. 'I haven't hunted for years.'

There was something in his voice that I couldn't pin down. It was almost like resentment. When I asked him why he had given up hunting, he said, 'I don't know.' And when he had recovered his equilibrium, he said, 'There isn't time for it, I suppose.' It was the restoration of his voice to its normal languorous tone that gave the game away. I had seen him with his guard down for the first time.

I said, 'You could probably have the odd day on my aunt's horse if you like. He's a bit skittish, but he's probably up to your weight.'

'Thanks,' he said. But he said it in a way that closed the subject, and I understood it as a refusal.

'Any time,' I said, and I turned towards the window to watch the weather. There was a big storm that day, and it was so dark outside that vision was restricted to a few feet and it was hard to say whether it was day or night. The thunder and lightning started at about the same time as a history lesson began, the history master's voice rumbling at a tone just above that of the rain.

When I looked back towards Smallgods I saw that he was reading James Joyce, thinly disguised by Chapters Six and Seven of *The Making of Modern Ireland*. And although he was completely intent on *Finnegan's Wake*, he looked up once or twice to check on the droning master, and when he caught my eye there was a conspiratorial grin, and he muttered something about Romantic Ireland being dead and gone and with O'Connell in Chapter Seven. Even though I didn't feel like it, I smiled back at him, because I was supposed to understand his jokes.

Mulally looked over our shoulders and saw what Smallgods was reading, and the clever expression on his face. 'Jasus, Temple,' he hissed, 'you're some eegit.'

Mulally was destined for Bolton Street. It was a wonder he could tear himself away from his own studying for the minute it took to criticise Smallgods. But Smallgods only turned and transfixed the unsqueezed acne spot on Mulally's chin for a few seconds. He didn't need to say anything to defend himself, because he did it by playing the white man. That was what they liked least: when he looked at them as though he knew something which they never could.

That was one of the days that Smallgods had brought lunch with him. As he unwrapped the package, Mulally howled, 'Jesus Christ, what's that smell?'

Smallgods bit into one of his delicate little sandwiches and we sniffed the air. There was something foreign and pungent in it.

'It's coming from you two,' Mulally said. He leaned over us and pointed to the sandwiches. 'What's in them?'

Smallgods swallowed what was in his mouth, and said, 'Tomato salad.'

Mulally clapped his hand over his face. 'There's something quare in those sandwiches.'

'I expect it is the garlic,' Smallgods said.

'Garlic!' By then there was a small crowd around the desk. In those days, garlic was only known in Kilnure by its reputation. They erupted: 'How could you eat that class of a thing?'

Smallgods was looking pleased with himself. 'Delicious,' he said.

Somehow they came to the conclusion that the only reason he could be eating garlic in his sandwiches was as an act of olfactory terrorism. There were people saying that he should be made to fucking eat it outside. Then Mulally snatched the packet and rolled it into a ball and canted it across the room, where somebody headbutted it back again. Within seconds, six or seven of them were playing football with Smallgods' lunch, jeering at him at the same time. He said nothing, but took out *Finnegan's Wake* and went back to his reading. Later they planted the packet in one of the other classrooms, like a bomb, and one of the masters refused to teach in that room until the source of the smell had been discovered and eliminated.

When things had quietened down, McGuire began to scrawl his daily piece of graffito on the blackboard. Because that was about the time of the dirty protests at Long Kesh, the drawing was, predictably, of an angry fist crushing an H-shaped Union Jack, with 'SMASH H BLOCKS NOW!' written beneath it.

I said something to Smallgods, but he wasn't listening. Instead, he was intent on the drawing that was emerging on the blackboard. His head was to one side, and his face bore an expression of irritation. When he finally spoke, his voice was measured.

'That Union Jack is wrong.'

McGuire stepped back from his handiwork. It had been improving steadily in the few weeks he had been drawing it, and he thought it was rather good. He had a banner at home which he was going to paint with the same logo, for carrying through the streets of Dublin in the marches. It expressed for him what was wrong with the world and his solution. He was someone who was so intense that he hardly ever spoke (or washed), and when he did say something it was through clenched teeth, the way he thought a freedom fighter would speak.

He said, 'What's wrong with it? Its only the fuckin' British flag anyway.'

Smallgods said, 'My point exactly. It isn't. It isn't the British flag at all. There is no cross of St Patrick. If your intention is to crush the Union, that flag defeats your purpose.'

McGuire said, 'Wouldn't you get the gist of it anyway?'

Smallgods shrugged, and they both looked at the flag for a while, until McGuire said what Smallgods had been waiting for him to say. 'Anyway, out of interest, how would you put it right?'

'Ah now,' Smallgods said, mocking the way McGuire spoke. 'I couldn't be telling you that. I don't think it is such a good idea to smash Long Kesh. All those nasty terrorists would escape and, you have to admit, if people choose to coat themselves in shit, they are hardly fit for decent society.'

Mulally hissed, 'You fucking Westbrit.'

Smallgods smiled at him as if it was a compliment, and stood up. He crossed the room and left it with provocative slowness while various people were calling him a Westbrit and a traitor, and after he was gone they began to laugh at him, ridiculing him. That was when I realised that the argument had nothing to do with politics. I followed him out.

CHRISTMAS

The Christmas tide came in and swept us out of school. Smallgods went away to some Zanzibar of his, and I stayed home for long sleepy Masses and heavy meals and crowded hunting. It seemed that nothing had changed between that Christmas and the one before it, and even that no time had elapsed in between. We were drugged by the tyranny of the season.

On Christmas Eve I came back from feeding the sheep out on the headland to find a flashy blonde girl sitting bareback on my horse in the middle of the yard, with Gerard holding on to the halter. My brother was being insufferable, on his best, most seductive behaviour, saying knowledgeable things about the horse when anyone could see that this was the closest he had been to one in the last ten years. His hair was shaven at the temples and the ponytail was dyed orange. He turned to me in a sneering sort of way as I climbed down from the tractor, and tried to overcome his lack of stature by introducing me as his baby brother. The girl, it seemed, was called Sarah.

I thought it was the last straw; that she was some trashy secretary from his record company whom he had inveigled to come down with him for Christmas so that they could smooch in front of the television, and he could flaunt his adulthood. Among the things that Gerard wouldn't forgive me for was the fact that I had grown to be tall and gangly, while he took after my mother's side of the family.

I looked critically at the horse's legs. It wasn't that I

thought they might have injured him, but I wanted to put them in their place, as amateurs. I said, 'It's cold. He should have a rug on him.'

'Too right,' she said. She threw her leg over his neck and slid down him. She was too careless and cheerful to be a secretary, and I thought she must be something worse: some punk starlet whom everyone had heard of, except me. A bigger feather in Gerard's cap.

There was something masculine in the way she put her hand out to shake mine. 'Pleased to meet you, John,' she said. 'What's the horse's name? Gerard here couldn't remember.'

Her accent was odd, even for a punk starlet.

'You're from Australia,' I said.

'How did you guess?' she said. Despite her affiliation to Gerard I started to like her.

I said, 'He's called Oedipus, from Ballingsaggard.'

She laughed and Gerard didn't. I took hold of the horse's halter and led him away to his box. I was still cross with Gerard for using my horse for showing off to his girl-friends.

When I found Dervla she was up to her elbows in the entrails of a turkey that was nearly as big as herself, humming that awful song about the boughs with holly. She said, 'John G., you must be famished. There's an apple tart in the fridge. I'll warm a bit to keep you going until your tea.'

'Who's Gerard's floozie?' I said.

'What?' she said. 'No. Sarah? No. Sarah isn't Gerard's girlfriend. She's your third cousin or something. I think. She's over here on holiday. She only phoned this morning. I told her to come here for Christmas. She was in a youth hostel. Imagine Christmas in a youth hostel. Could you not have taken your boots off in the porch? Although I suppose Australians are used to spending Christmas in strange places. Shark-infested beaches. She's seeing the world. I suppose that's what Australians do. I sent her to look at the horses.

She said she's been sitting on brumbies half her life. I suppose I could give her a day on Odysseus. Though I don't think I have anything her size to wear. But I don't think Australians care about dressing up for that sort of thing. Shit, John G., I've cut half my finger off. Can you feed the mare for me when you feed the others? Where's the plasters? Feck.'

That was Dervla. People had been saying for the past four or five years that my father should marry her. It was thought unfair to deny her the chance of a husband when one was so easily available. In the minds of those people marriage would have been the just reward for her long years of patient service; and an appropriate source of comfort for my father after all his suffering. But I don't think that he and Dervla liked each other: he thanked her conscientiously after every meal, and she tended to direct her conversation to me. I think that part of the problem may have been that it was hard to find fault with someone as self-sacrificing as Dervla was. You were never in a position to fight with her, and when she lost her temper you could only apologise. That wasn't likely to give her much satisfaction either.

While she was looking for the plasters, I said, 'Where's the biscuits? I may bring them round to Stasia now.'

Dervla had the tin of biscuits already wrapped in Christmas paper. It was my chief duty on Christmas Eve to go down the road to Stasia Dwyer with her present. It was always the same brand of biscuits in the same tin.

Stasia had been bedridden for thirty years, and lived in a small cottage at the edge of the farm with her bachelor son, Mikey, who mostly lived on the dole, with a bit of salmon poaching on the side.

'God save ye,' Mikey said when I knocked and went into the cottage. He was looking very spruce, having just shaved for Midnight Mass. In the normal course of events he only shaved on Saturday night for Mass on Sunday morning. I know that protocol demanded I reply with 'God save all here' but I could never bring myself to do that.

My face reddened, and I said, 'Hiya.'

He brought me through to his mother, who was propped up in a big brass bed with the Sacred Heart over it and a stick of holly pushed behind the eternal lamp. On the table by her bed there were bottles of pills and beefeater dolls in plastic tubes from the Tower of London, and a picture of the three Kennedy boys. Mikey shouted, 'Mam!' at her to wake her up from her doze.

'Happy Christmas, Mrs Dwyer,' I said and put the tin of biscuits on the bed.

'Mikey,' she said. 'Oh, John G. Mikey, turn that television off when there's visitors. John G., Happy Christmas to you, boy. Will you look at the size of him. It's so long since I saw you. You must be as big as your daddy now. Huge. Isn't he huge, Mikey?'

Mikey had gone to the television in the corner of the room. He hadn't turned it off, but had turned the volume down, and was watching it.

'Huge,' he said.

When I was a child I was obliged to kiss her at Christmas, and she liked to tease me about it still. 'Where's me Christmas kiss, boy?'

'I have a bit of a cold on me,' I said. 'I wouldn't like to pass it on. You're keeping well.'

She was shredding the wrapping paper from the biscuits. 'Isn't that lovely,' she said. 'I remember well, your poor mother, God rest her, got me these biscuits the first time I had them.'

'You're looking well,' I said. I knew if I got her to talk about her health, the conversation would be safe enough, and I wouldn't have to say anything more.

'The pains are terrible,' she said. 'The doctor was with me yesterday. I hates getting him to come out, but Mikey called him.' She was off.

I relaxed for the next ten minutes, and when I thought I had been there for a respectable amount of time, I said,

'Dad said to say he'll be in on his way to Midnight Mass, and Dervla will be in tomorrow morning.'

My father would call and spend at least two hours talking to her, which he did regularly, and Dervla would come round with a Christmas dinner for her and Mikey. She knew all that already, but it was my signal that I was leaving.

Back in their kitchen, Mikey made me wait while he took a brace of pheasants from the back door and wrapped them in newspaper. On the dresser there was a stack of identical biscuit tins, one for every year; and Christmas cards from England were set out over the fire.

Desperate for something to say, I said, 'We have an Australian girl staying. She might be just the job for you.'

Mikey gave me a lewd wink. 'Send her round,' he said. 'Send her round and I'll fix her for you.'

I was woken in the middle of the night by my father playing Santa Claus. The phosphorescent hands on the new alarm clock said a quarter past three. He was hanging a big white stocking on the post at the end of my bed. It would have mandarin oranges and chocolates in it, and probably a new pair of riding gloves. Then I drifted back to sleep again.

In the morning I took my stocking and went to Gerard's room. It was hard to wake him, even after I had drawn the curtains.

'Fuck that,' he said.

'Happy Christmas,' I said. 'Open your stocking.'

'Fuck that. What time is it?'

I sat on his bed and emptied my stocking. As well as the usual things there was a pair of spurs. 'What did you get?' I said.

Gerard swore again and turned his face into the pillow, so I emptied his stocking out for him. 'Look what you got,' I said.

'John G., you're a bollix.' He propped himself on an elbow to look at his present. It was a silk tie with blue spots, the sort that bankers wear. 'The man is mad,' he said. 'What did he give you?'

I held up the spurs and the gloves.

He said, 'I should have known. At least the fucker put some thought into what he gave you. I should wrap the tie up and give it back to him for his present.'

'Why?' I said. 'What did you get him?'

'Nothing. I forgot.'

I tried to think what I had that I could wrap for my father and pretend was from Gerard. The diary, perhaps, would be the best thing.

Gerard said, 'There's only one thing to do this early in the morning on a day like this.' He put his arm beneath the bed and pulled a bag out, from which he took an enormous lump of dope. 'Christmas present from myself to myself. An ounce and a half of the best,' he said. 'It's nearly time you learned to do this.'

Since it was Christmas, I thought I should try it, but I only ended up coughing and choking and spluttering. Gerard said, 'The good things in life never come easily. I'll put a lump in your pudding later. That'll get you going.'

He got out of bed to go to the bathroom. There was real horror in my voice when I said, 'What? You sleep with no clothes on.'

'Jesus Christ, John G.,' he said. 'Grow up.'

Christmas dinner was easier than usual because of the diary, and Sarah from Australia. My father kept telling Gerard that a diary was just the thing he needed, and Gerard was actually smiling back at him. I didn't know at the time that Gerard was smiling because of the dope. Sarah kept up a cheerful monologue about her adventures in the capitals of Europe and the jungles of Asia, while Dervla fed her questions and repeated that it was wonderful what a young girl could do nowadays.

In our house, after the main courses, we had Christmas

pudding and then the sherry trifle, before the cake. As she tackled her trifle, Sarah said, 'This is amazing; all this food. Your mother is a wonderful cook.'

The remark was addressed to me. 'My mother,' I said.

There was complete silence around the table. Dervla and my father had a frozen look about them, and Gerard was smiling more intensely. Sarah was still looking at me as though she was waiting for an answer.

'Dervla isn't my mother,' I said.

My father recovered himself. 'My wife is dead, God rest her soul.'

Then Dervla launched herself. 'I'm his aunt,' she said, and cut through Sarah's apologies, talking about her as if she wasn't there. 'The poor girl wasn't to know. A bishop could have made the same mistake. There's no need to apologise. Jesus Christ, I bit my tongue. That's what you get for trying to talk when there's food in your mouth. Are you finished that trifle, John G.? I'll go and make the tea and bring the cake in. Would anyone like another glass of milk first?'

As she left the room with the trifle bowls she glared at Gerard, whose head was resting in his hand while he giggled like a half-wit.

After the cake had been dealt with, I said that I would go and feed the sheep, and Sarah broke her silence to ask if she could come with me. We found her some Wellingtons and she stood on the back of the tractor, getting down to open the gates. By the time we had reached the headland she was back to her cheerful self, fooling around and laughing as she held the gates open. As we emptied the feed into the troughs and broke the bales open she got me talking about the sheep. She knew a lot about them because she lived on a sheep farm. Then we walked out to the top of the headland to look at the river.

'What are all those flowers?' she said.

I said, 'When the gorse is out of bloom, kissing is out of season.'

She laughed and thumped me on the shoulder, and we went down to the marshes. The next-door farmer had taken a grant from the Common Market to drain his marshes and grow corn on them, and had built a huge bank by the river to keep the water out. But the water had seeped through and the drained land was now a vast shallow lake, and the bank had become a long isthmus of green between the stagnant and the flowing water. We walked this bank, looking over at County Waterford and the yellow furze on the other side.

She said, 'So what's the story about your mother? I could have died in there.'

'Sorry,' I said. 'She was very sick. She died. Dervla's been looking after us since I was a baby.'

I sat on a rock that was big enough for two and sinking into the soft bank and wouldn't be there in another few years. I sat on it as if I wanted to look at the river. Sarah sat beside me.

'I'm sorry,' she said. 'What did she die of?' She wasn't going to let up.

'She was mad. She went mad after I was born, and when I was about eleven she died. I don't know if she committed suicide. She probably did, because no one talks about it. But maybe she didn't. Apparently it's hard to kill yourself in a mental home. They watch you all the time.'

I wasn't upset by what I was saying. I was hardly aware that I was saying it. My nose was full of the smell of coconut, but I couldn't tell whether it was from the furze across the river or from Sarah's shampoo. Being that close to Sarah was making me feel uncomfortable, and at the same time I wanted to get closer still. She had her arm around my shoulders, to comfort me, I suppose. But there was an awkward tightening in my trousers.

'Do you want to talk about it?' she said.

I said that I didn't mind, and turned my face towards hers, and then we were kissing, just as I had been wondering what kissing was like.

'Your hands are warm,' she said.

'I'm always warm,' I said.

And then the kissing got serious. She tasted of nicotine and cheery lipsalve and Christmas cake, and her hands were kneading my shoulder-blades. My arm brushed her breast and I apologised, but she said that it was all right, and took my hand and put it up beneath her jersey. She said it was just as well that I had warm hands, but I was hardly listening. Something extraordinary was happening. I wanted to put my hand into my trousers to adjust myself because I had become so uncomfortable, but I was hoping that she wouldn't notice that I had an erection, so I couldn't draw attention to it. And then my hand found her breast, and there was something hard on the end of it. I wasn't expecting that. I knew that girls had nipples, but I didn't know that they could harden.

At first I thought the extraordinary thing that was happening had something to do with Gerard's dope. I wondered if he had slipped some into my pudding after all. And then I thought I was dying. My head was exploding. I wondered if the excitement was giving me a heart attack. All my muscles contracted and I slipped off the rock on to the grass with a groan.

Sarah was laughing, and I thought: The bitch has killed me and now she's laughing. And then I felt wet in my trousers and I thought that was the final indignity: that I had pissed myself on my deathbed.

It wasn't until I got the smell of pyjamas that I knew what had happened. I swear to God that that had never happened to me before in my waking hours. I suppose I may have been a late developer.

I said that we should go back. She was feeling the hair on the back of my head, but I was too embarrassed to respond. I couldn't look her in the eye. She held on to the back of my jacket as we climbed the headland.

She said, 'So what does the G. stand for?'

'The what?'

'Why do they call you John G.?'

I had never met anyone so unafraid of asking personal questions before. Except Smallgods Temple maybe. And the tone she was using implied that she had a right to an answer. As if making me pollute myself had given her the right to know.

'There was another baby between Gerard and me. He was called John, so I had to be called John G., or it would have been bad luck.'

'What happened to him?'

I had had enough. I stopped and turned to her and said, 'The angels came and took him away to be with Baby Jesus in heaven.'

She was searching my face to see whether she was supposed to laugh or not. But I wasn't giving anything away.

'All right,' she said. 'I get it.'

She let go of my jacket and walked ahead of me towards the tractor. By the time I caught up with her, I felt so bad about it that I told her I was sorry. And instantly she said that no, she was sorry. She put her arms around me beneath my jacket and pushed me back against the tractor wheel. I was just about to kiss her again when there was the sound of footsteps in the mud, and a voice called out.

'Grand evening now.' It was Mikey. He was walking from the direction of the marshes. I knew by the way he was leering that he had been watching us down there.

'Grand,' I said.

It would be all over the parish by the morning. I was glad that things hadn't gone any further than they had. Sarah was looking at my red face and laughing again.

She said. 'Do you mind if I come to your room tonight?'

'There might be a problem there.'

I couldn't tell her that I still slept with my father. I couldn't suggest that I go to her room, because there was only a thin wall between that and Dervla's.

'All right,' she said. 'I see.'

She was sulking now, and there was nothing I could say. I drove the tractor so badly on the way back that it nearly overturned on the hill.

She went away the next day. She had arranged to meet some people in Istanbul. But before she went, she said that I should come and see her in Australia, any time.

JANUARY

Smallgods was stranger. Christmas seemed to have worn him badly. He was thinner in the face and his eyes were sunk deeper and seemed paler. When he wasn't talking, a muscle raced up and down his jawbone all the time. I wanted to ask him whether he did it deliberately, and whether he had had to practise it for a long time to get such definition. I tried flexing my own jaw muscles to see if I could develop them to the same extent, but I couldn't remember to keep it up. But Smallgods had a different sort of jaw from mine; one of those square ones that would become jowly in middle age.

When it wasn't raining and we had art classes, we went sketching in the churchyard, or the fields above the river, or anywhere quiet. Moran the mad art mistress was away on honeymoon. She had stolen our hearts and then deserted us to marry a farmer. When she came back she would have a different name. We had thought of her as one of us, and it was odd now to think of one of us being married.

If you went sketching without a wristwatch it was easy to lose track of time and miss geography and maths and turn up at lunchtime with a bewildered look saying, 'Good heavens, is that the time?' By some wonderful fluke both Smallgods and I had lost our watches and so had simplified our school lives. St Joseph's churchyard was the best place for this ruse. You were invisible from the street, and because it was Protestant nobody ever went there. The church was medieval, now partly in ruins, with the core of it over-restored by the Victorians in keeping with the austerity of the lowest of

Protestants. It was locked most of the time, but now and again the verger would appear and bring us in to see the wooden box pews and the stacks of bibles and the plain white ceiling.

Outside in the churchyard and in the ruins, sarcophagi from before the Reformation littered the ground; reliefs of men who would have fought with Strongbow etched in Caen sandstone and half covered with ivy. You couldn't help thinking that things looked better half destroyed.

It might have been a Tuesday. Does it matter? It was brittle cold weather: the nearest we got to a proper winter that year. Smallgods was hard at work, sketching the lichen that covered a Norman woman's face. He somehow managed to make the whole thing look more intimidating than the sculptor had perhaps intended. I was lying stretched out in the open sarcophagus below and thinking about the myth that if you dared to lie in that coffin the lid would come crashing down off the wall and kill you stone dead. There was no sign of it moving. I was thinking about Sarah too, and wondering if it was love or not, to be thinking about her so much, and to have an erection half the time; and whether I would end my days married to her in Boogiwarra, W.A. Or whether she would end her days married to me by the river in Roscarmony.

Boogiwarra seemed the more exciting possibility, with mobs of sheep and blowies and farming on a motor bike instead of a tractor. And kissing in the heat, and life without so many clothes on. There might be a problem with kissing in short trousers. I flinched to think how I had embarrassed myself, and wondered what might have happened if I had gone to her room. I thought it couldn't be natural to be thinking about sex so much, so I opened my eyes and tried to concentrate on reading the inscription around the face that Smallgods was drawing. It was difficult, upside-down, and in Latin.

'*Hic jacet* Elizabeth Roth. She's no oil painting, that one.'

'What?' Smallgods said.

'Listen?' I said. 'Tell me. Listen?'

'Listen, listen? The cat is pissin'.'

'No, seriously, tell us. Did you ever do it with any-one?'

'I'm saving myself for a widow with a pub,' he said.

'But would you if you weren't married?'

'For Christ's sake, John G. Moore,' he said. 'Stop worrying about it. Big blond boys like you don't stay virgins for long. When someone asks you to do it, you'll do it.'

I didn't see what the colour of my hair had to do with it, and said so.

'Blonds have no morals,' he said. 'It's well known. When did you last see a blond priest? You're headed for a life of debauchery.'

'That must be it, so,' I said.

I almost believed him for a moment, and then I remem-bered that I had already said no to Sarah. I watched him for a while, and decided that he looked far from innocent himself. He had the face of someone who had met the devil. But then Christ must have had the face of some-one who had met the devil. But neither was Christ an innocent.

'Did you ever wonder if you were the Messiah?' I said.

'I still do. How did you guess?' It was hard to know if he was being serious.

'Hey, Temple, do your people have pucks of money or something?'

'Why?'

'I can't imagine what you will do for a living.'

'I hear they're looking for a Messiah. Does it matter?'

'I thought you could buy the farm next door to ours and we could be neighbouring farmers till the day we die.'

'Or I could wash dishes. It doesn't matter. If you get prosperous I'll come and live in your attic and write the definitive novel. Or paint seminal pictures. I don't know.

I could end up in the British Army. In my grandfather's regiment.'

'You wouldn't last five minutes.'

'Free hunting at Melton Mowbray.'

'Go scratch yourself.'

FEBRUARY

February began about the middle of the month. By February I mean the best time of year, when it isn't cold any longer, and the ditches are impregnated with dampness from a constant drizzle, and you begin to watch for signs of buds on the trees.

I had gone out in the morning without a coat on so that the rain soaked through all my clothes, to the skin. You do that sort of thing when you are seventeen, and you enjoy it.

Dervla ranted at me, and threatened to keep me home from school in case I had caught a cold.

'I don't mind,' I said.

So then she decided to punish me by sending me to school, and I nearly said that I didn't mind that either. But it was coming perilously close to giving her cheek. It wasn't the giving of cheek that worried me, but the guilt afterwards. Dervla should have been a religion.

Smallgods had a new pair of shoes on him. They were very old-fashioned, but they looked new because they had such a shine.

'I think they were my grandfather's,' he said. 'I found them in the attic.'

I thought: That's what it must be like to be rich and grand. You don't care what anyone thinks, because you can find better things in your attic than anyone else could find in a shop. Smallgods' mother picked him up from school in a battered Renault van, and he got into it as if it was a Rolls-Royce. When my father collected me in the BMW, I found myself wincing at the vulgarity of it. I told him he should always pick me up in the Landrover, but when he asked me why I couldn't explain it to him.

I looked in our own attic, and found nothing but rubbish, and a lot of clothes that must have been my mother's, in cardboard trunks and mothballs.

MARCH

The mildness of February was gone, and it might as well have been winter again for the hardness that was blowing in the wind. I was out on the bicycle, on the tiny roads between Roscarmony and Ballynell. Jim the postman had given me the directions to get there.

'You'll know it by the long low wall and the bollards by the gate and there's a fierce amount of big oak trees by the house itself and sure God you can't miss it now.' Then Jim stuck a finger in his ear and asked me how Dervla was and wasn't it a fright you could break a leg as easy as that, the Lord bless us and save us.

I said that the Lord might if he had nothing better to do, but either that remark was lost on Jim, or he had the graciousness to ignore it.

He said that it wouldn't be long till the summer now, please God, and he revved the engine of his orange van and drove out of the yard.

Dervla had been kicked by her brood mare, and her leg was broken in two places. It made it easier for me to get away from the house for a few hours without having to explain anything. I took the bicycle instead of one of the cars so that she wouldn't hear me leaving.

The roads were so winding that sometimes they almost came back on themselves. Someone said it was because Wexford had had such conscientious landlords during the famine. Instead of allowing their tenants to starve, they gave them work building completely unnecessary roads. The distances were doubled for the sake of the hungry.

Smallgods hadn't come to school for more than a fortnight. The last day he was in, he had announced that he wasn't taking Irish as a subject any more. We had always been told that it was compulsory, but he had looked up the regulations and found a loophole. No one had seen him since. I decided to go and find out what had happened to him. It was Sunday, after Mass.

From the top of a hill, I looked down on a squat dark house surrounded by oak trees. It looked like the description of Ballynell, but I wondered if it could be, because it looked so deserted. The river came within two or three hundred yards of it. I thought that if I had borrowed Mikey Dwyer's boat I would have been there quicker. But then I would have had to explain to Mikey where I was going.

The River Barrow was supposed to be sinister below Kilnure. It was cursed to take three lives every year. But they were nearly all suicides, and I saw nothing sinister in that. The river provided a way out for those who wanted it. It was better than the other traditional method in our area, which was to park in a lane and put a hose from your exhaust pipe through the car window. That was the farmers' way of doing it. The townspeople threw themselves in the river.

When I reached the low wall and the bollards, I could hear the crowing of bantam cocks. I knew they were bantams, because Smallgods had told me that he had a pet bantam that was supposed to look like me. Apparently it was gawky with a tuft of white feathers on the top of its head. I wasn't sure about being compared to a chicken, but I suppose it was better than not being noticed at all.

There was a long straight drive with a bad surface, and at the end of it a dachshund stood guard, raising her hackles. Behind her, a thin black gundog, not much more than a puppy, sloped around, sniffing the hens' backsides. As I came nearer, the dachshund set up a vicious barking, and the gundog sat down and howled in sympathy, without knowing what the alarm was.

I stopped just short of the dogs. The dachshund looked like a biter. A small child came over and asked me my name. As it spoke, it put one arm round the neck of the gundog, and thrust the other arm half-way down the animal's throat. The child could have been of either sex, and had orange hair; it was no more than six years old. A bantam came over and began to peck at the child's shoelaces, while the gundog salivated ecstatically.

'John,' I said.

'Huh,' the child said.

The surface of the yard was broken and more mud than gravel. The stable doors were off their hinges and the roofs more hole than tile. I thought I must have come to the wrong place. The house looked as though no one had lived in it for years, with mould half-way up the back door. But there was smoke coming from the chimneys.

'Does that dog bite?' I said.

'She will if I tell her to.' I thought that this child couldn't possibly be a relation of Smallgods. But still, at the back of its broad Wexford accent, there was a superior intonation that was familiar. And it looked at me as though it knew something that I didn't.

Its attention was fixed on my bicycle lamp.

'Does that yoke work?'

'Yes,' I said. 'But there aren't any batteries in it.'

'You should get a dynamo, so.'

The fowl at its feet had opened one set of shoelaces and started on the other.

'Are you a little Temple?' I said. 'Is this place Ballynell?'

The child looked at me as though I was an idiot.

I tried again. 'Does Godfrey Temple live here?'

'Are you his friend?'

'I suppose so.' I thought I was getting somewhere at last.

Then the child said, 'Smallgods told me about you. You're the one that looks like his chicken. Are you a Protestant?'

That threw me. 'No,' I said. 'What makes you think that?'

'Oldgods said that Smallgods was only a bloody Protestant, and all his bloody friends were Protestants. He was nearly as mad as when I let the dog in and he did a shit on the sofa. That was after he told Father Apple he was an eegit and wouldn't go to Mass.'

'Who did?'

'Smallgods did. I said could I stay home from Mass too, but I still have to make my communion at Easter.'

'That's nice,' I said. I decided that Smallgods and Oldgods were probably the child's imaginary friends; that perhaps the poor child wasn't the whole shilling.

'It's not nice. I have to wear a bloody dress.'

So the child was a girl.

'Listen,' I said, 'listen?'

'The cat is pissin',' she said.

That was when I knew she had to be a Temple. I decided to negotiate my way past the dachshund and knock at the back door. The child was patiently trying to make the chicken stand on the gundog's back, while the dog, with his mouth closed about the child's knee, was growling contentedly.

'Stand still, you cunt you,' she said. I didn't know whether she was referring to me or the dog or the chicken.

'That's not a nice way to talk,' I said.

'Huh,' she said. And then she narrowed her eyes. 'If you tell on me, I'll make the dog bite you.'

'I promise. I won't tell. Is there anyone else around? Is Godfrey here?'

'The oul wan and the Deadlies are in the kitchen. If you hop up on that yoke you can see them through the window.' She was pointing at a dilapidated mounting block under a huge window, dark with dirt.

With a great deal of apprehension, I went over to the

window and looked through it. Beyond the dusty glass there were shadows moving in the gloom. It was impossible to tell anything about them, except that they seemed to be female. With my preconceptions about Smallgods' grandness, I thought they might all be kitchen maids.

The child said, 'Stay there!' Again I wasn't sure if she meant the animals or me. 'I'll tell 'em you're here.'

She went to the mouldy back door and pushed it open nine inches, and shouted, 'Hey! There's a man here on a bicycle.'

A voice inside asked her who it was.

'I don't know,' she said. 'Some friend of Smallgods. But not very bright, if you know what I mean.'

The figures beyond the murky window were standing on tiptoe and looking out at me, and the child turned around, with a feint trace of a smile for the first time, and with a hint of charm.

'The oul wan says come in,' she said as she walked past me, and went across the yard with the chicken under her arm, both of them eating the same currant bun which she had pulled from her pocket. The gundog hoovered the crumbs up behind them.

When I turned back towards the house the mouldy door was fully opened by another girl. She was a proper girl, with a skirt and brushed long hair; perhaps fifteen years old. Three more dachshunds came racing out from behind her as if they were going to devour me. They formed a sort of knot about my ankles, and the girl shouted at them, and whistled, and asked me to come inside.

The kitchen of Ballynell was vast, with a window that did nothing to light it at each end. A single electric bulb hung from the ceiling, but still it took seconds to adjust to the darkness, and scan the room, and work out which was the furniture and which the people.

A female voice came out of the dispersing gloom and said, 'Hello,' and, sensing that it was not a malign voice,

I returned the greeting, in the same tone of noncommittal warmth.

The woman who had spoken looked like an overbred lurcher. She was long and too thin and moved as though she might be neurotic. She stood at the end of a wooden table that was strewn with flour and tins and butter. Six girls stood around the table, three down each side: two who looked like Temple, two who looked like the woman, one who had fair hair, and one who looked like no one. It was a bit like a factory production line.

I neither knew how to explain myself, nor why I was there when I could have been at home with the horses. I was embarrassed by having seven pairs of feminine eyes looking at me at the same time, and not four of them the same colour.

'I'm sorry,' I said. 'Is Godfrey here?'

The woman asked one of the girls to see if Smallgods was in his room. I was beginning to be unnerved at that stage by all the references to small gods. And then, as a deft conversation filler, she asked me how I had got there. She said she hadn't heard a car.

'I cycled over. It isn't far. From Roscarmony.'

'Roscarmony?' she said. 'You aren't a Moore, are you?'

When I said that I was, she began to exclaim with great goshes and good heavens that there couldn't still be Moores at Roscarmony, and she knew my father well and my grandfather. She said something about tennis parties in the fifties, and the heady days before the roads were tarred.

The great goshes and good heavens, and the way she addressed her children as darling, made her seem almost like an Englishwoman, but you could tell that she wasn't English really, from the way she softened her double t's, and didn't wear a wristwatch, or smile all the time the way the English do. And her windows were dirty, but she wasn't a hippy, so she couldn't be English.

The girl reappeared with Smallgods in tow. He was deeply

tanned, but when he saw me the colour left his face. He seemed uncertain what to do, and I had a surge of panic, and wanted to rush out of the house and bicycle away as fast as I could.

But it can't have been for more than a second. He burst into a smile. I had never seen so much genuine pleasure in his face before.

'Hiya,' he said, and I suppose I said the same thing back. Then there was an awkward silence.

'Smallgods, darling,' the woman said. 'Would you like to take your friend into the sitting-room? He'll get covered in flour in here.'

'I'm sorry,' he said. But instead of taking me away, he introduced me to his mother and all his sisters. He did it in a formal way that made me feel at a disadvantage. All the girls had archaic Irish names, and I was obliged to shake hands with them. It wasn't until after that ceremony that I was led to the sitting-room.

I said, 'Well you aren't dead anyway.'

'Not yet,' he said. 'I'll make you some tea. I won't be long.'

I was left alone in their sitting-room, which was nothing like ours. There were no ornaments, and instead of a carpet there was a badly worn rug on the floor. Some of the armchairs had blankets thrown over them because the fabric beneath had given way, and they all faced towards a dusty television. I placed myself in a hollow between two springs on the sofa and waited for the tea.

When he returned, I said, 'I tried to telephone, but I couldn't find you in the book.'

'We don't have a telephone,' he said. 'Sorry about all that.' He nodded towards the kitchen. 'Oldgods just got some money, so my mother is filling the freezer.'

That was when I got him to explain all the Smallgods and Oldgods stuff, and the Deadlies. He had seven sisters, one for each of the Deadly Sins.

'So who's the one with the red hair outside?'

'Wrath,' he said.

'So who is lust? And gluttony?'

'We aren't as awful as that,' he said. 'Wrath is Wrath because her real name is so terrible that if you use it she'll set the dogs on you. The others are only the Deadlies collectively. We do it to annoy Oldgods. Wrath is my pet.'

'So where did you get the tan? I thought you were dead.'

He laughed at me, but it seemed I had somehow flattered him.

'Skiing. In Italy.'

'That must have been nice for you,' I said.

He was still laughing at me. 'Having you around is like having a wife,' he said.

Through the window I could see Wrath in the yard. She was poking at a drain with a big stick. Then she let a delighted scream out of her as a rat broke cover near her feet, and she and all the dogs set off in pursuit of it. There was the sound of a car in the distance. Wrath stopped in her tracks and called the dogs back. They obeyed her meekly, and they all disappeared behind the farm buildings.

'Oh God,' Smallgods said.

'What?'

'Wrath is our early-warning system.'

'For what?'

'You'll see.'

The car pulled up in the yard. A bearded man got out of it and came into the house. A minute later he came into the room where we were sitting.

'*Dia dhaoibh*,' he said.

He was tight-lipped under his beard, which covered a jaw even squarer than Smallgods'. There was a *fáinne* in his lapel; that is: the badge by which Irish speakers recognise one another in the street.

Smallgods rolled his eyes to heaven at me, but so the

man couldn't see. The muscles in his jaws were working like pistons.

He said, '*Je veux présenter mon père. Mon ami, John Moore. John a eu la gentillesse de venir voir si je vais bien. Il a regretté mon absence a l'école.*'

His father said something in Irish, but it was so rapid that I couldn't catch it. Even if I had, I wouldn't have known which language to answer in. And the atmosphere that the man had brought into the room with him would have been enough to silence me on its own. Seeing my bewilderment, he spoke to me very slowly, asking if I spoke Irish.

'*An bhfuil gáeilge agat, tú féin?*'

'Ahm,' I said. After thirteen years of learning the language in school, I couldn't think of a single word of it. '*Tá.* I mean. Well, a bit.'

He looked at me as if I was subhuman, and then said something else to Smallgods, which Smallgods answered in French. The man grunted, and left the room.

Smallgods said, 'I told him that you wanted to go to the pub, so I suppose it would be as well if we did.'

'Fucksake,' I said. 'This is a madhouse.'

He got a second bicycle out of the shed, and contained himself until we were at the top of the drive. Then he pulled on his brakes and put his leg to the ground. His teeth were clenched.

'Bollix,' he said. The word was not normally in his vocabulary, except as a joke. There was no sign of a joke now. 'I'm not going to be able to stand this much longer.'

He was silent for the other mile and a half to the pub, looking at me now and again, in a speculative way. He was deciding whether to tell me or not.

Inside, the pub was completely yellow with smokestains, and we sat on two hard settles meeting at right-angles. Mrs Furlong had to be shouted for for ten minutes before she appeared and gave us a drink. Smallgods ordered two rum and blackcurrants without asking me what I wanted, but he looked over as he ordered it, seeking my approval. After Mrs Furlong had asked me how my father and Dervla were, she disappeared back into the house.

'So?' I said.

He said, 'I don't think you'll see me back at school. I've just decided to go away again.'

'To Italy?'

'Well, it might be better weather for hitching this time,' he said.

'You hitched?'

'How else can you get there with no money?' he said. He had two black lines curling up from his lips from the drink. I was choking on mine. That was my first taste of alcohol. I didn't like it, but I was prepared to allow that it might be an acquired taste, so I said nothing.

'My father is English,' he said. 'You know that. They are a peculiar race. He doesn't allow us to speak anything but Irish in his presence. He has ideals about reviving the language that only a foreigner could entertain. You remember, the last day I was in school, that I told them I was giving up Irish? Oldgods didn't take it too well when I told him. I suppose I shouldn't have told him in English. But I told him that I wasn't speaking Irish again, ever. The final straw was on the Sunday after Mass, when I argued with the parish priest about religion. It was quite a friendly argument, but Oldgods said afterwards that I had insulted him, and I had to apologise before I went to Mass again. So I said that was fine by me, since I had no intention of ever going to Mass again with an idiot like Father Apple supervising the proceedings. Anyway, he said that he couldn't have a heathen and a Protestant living in his house and giving a bad example to the children, so I took him at his word and hitch-hiked to Italy. It only took two days. It was a good time to be there. The mountains aren't far away.'

'So how come you're back?'

'We compromised. I have to speak to him in French or

Italian. Usually Italian, but I used French while you were there so you'd have a better chance of understanding it.'

'Thanks,' I said. 'You needn't have bothered.' I had finished half my drink, and was feeling a bit weak in the head. He interpreted my silence as a willingness to listen. He might as well have. I didn't mind listening.

'I've had enough,' he said. 'It's ridiculous being forced into this sort of childish behaviour by that man's fantasies and power-games. I'm going back to Dublin to find a flat and a job. It's about time I had some money. I've had it with living in poverty. And that school is a waste of time. I could pass the Leaving Certificate tomorrow if I took it.'

I was shaken from my stupor. 'Poverty?' I said. 'I thought you were rolling in it.'

He seemed surprised by my impression, although it was he who gave it to me. 'None of our family is exactly overweight,' he said. 'Are you drunk? You've only had half a drink.'

'I think so,' I said. 'I feel sick.'

I had to walk the bicycle the first two miles home before I felt well enough to mount it. Before we parted, he had said to me, 'I'll send you my address in Dublin as soon as I've got one. You can write to me. But don't be offended if I don't write back. I never write letters. It's the thought of all those biographers sifting through them in a hundred years' time. You could visit me, and I'll teach you to drink. Come up in the summer.'

As I left him I thought that would be it. I would probably never see him again. I was surprised how little I minded, considering how much I had missed him at school.

EASTER

The last day of the season we hunted close to Ballynell. It wasn't intended, but a fox led us for a six-mile point in the afternoon, and went to ground in a bank on the top of the hill that overlooked Smallgods' house. It was decided not to dig, and so Charlie was given the last laugh of the season. The hounds had chopped a fox earlier in the week, so there was no need to give them blood. We stood about, above the river, flushed and steaming with the long gallop. My father's cousin, Mary Howlin, was with me. Since Roscarmony was nearer than her horsebox, I thought I might hack home. She and I went down through the yard of Ballynell, but the hounds and the rest of the field went back the way they had come.

Wrath was in the yard. She had a dead grey rat by the tail, which she was swinging round her head to tease her black gundog, like a falconer with a lure.

When the horse came into the yard, Wrath dropped her rat to watch us. I stopped and said hello to her, but she didn't recognise me in hunting clothes.

I took my hat off, and said, 'It's me. Is Smallgods home?'

'Oh you,' she said. 'What's wrong with your horse's eye?'

'He's blind.'

I could see that the fact that I was riding a blind horse inflated me in her estimation. I kept a tight hold of the other rein so that she couldn't see his good eye. 'Is Smallgods around?'

'No,' she said. 'He's in Dublin.'

As we rode away, Mary Howlin asked me who the child was.

'The sister of someone I go to school with.'

Mary Howlin considered herself my father's oracle. She said, 'If I'd known there were people like that at your school, I would have made your dad send you away to board.'

She wiped the drip from the end of her nose with her glove, and glared back at the house. 'There used to be some very nice people living there. It's a great pity.'

APRIL

'Hey, Moore! Your friend is back.'

The classroom was full, and Cochran was over on the other side of it, by the window that looked towards the school gates.

'Don't be thick,' I said, because I thought he might be having a go at me.

I should have known that Cochran wouldn't have the wit to invent a lie like that. Smallgods strolled into the classroom a minute later, and sat in the desk next to me. He looked better than I had seen him look in a long time.

'How was Dublin?' I said.

'Very provincial,' he said. 'I thought I might as well be hung for a sheep as a lamb.'

MAY

The summer that the house fell down began on my birthday, while I was out looking for Clytemnestra, my aunt's vicious brood mare. As the mare's confinement approached, she had been installed in the paddock near the house, where Dervla could keep an eye on her from the back porch. Dervla's leg was still in plaster where the mare had kicked her in March, and she sat in the porch all day, spewing out hideous brown knitting and worrying about the expected foal.

My father and I had been to Waterford to get my present. I had surprised him by asking for a record player. Smallgods had introduced me to the rather depressing electronic music that was current. My father took it in his stride, but I could see him hoping that I wasn't going to go the same way as Gerard. He ended up forking out for quite a good system, because Smallgods came along to help choose it. Although he had no record player himself, Smallgods had very snobbish ideas about which brand of equipment one should have. Then we went to a record shop and brought all three Joy Division albums. 'That will do to get you going,' Smallgods said.

Back at Roscarmony, Dervla was in a state, hopping out to us on her crutches as soon as the car swung into the yard.

'She's gone an hour. She just broke the fence and went. Towards the small wood. Jesus, Dan, she might be at the bottom of the big drain by now. I knew I should have borrowed that pony off Mary to keep her company.'

'What,' my father said, 'and have a dead pony to pay for as well as the barley she's trampling?'

'I'll go and find her,' I said. 'She won't come to you.'

It was true that the mare was terrified of my father. She knew that he hated her. I hated her too, but she thought she could get away with it with me. Dervla was the only one who had any time for her, and Dervla was up to her hip in plaster of Paris for her weakness.

My father said, 'The only thing that mare is fit for is the factory.'

Dervla winced, but it might have been the pain of standing upright.

'Hurry up, John G.,' she said. 'She isn't due for another three weeks, but you never know. I have a terrible feeling.'

There was a drizzle as I set out across the fields with a halter. I was half disappointed when I got to the big drain and found that she wasn't dead at the bottom of it. I began to call out for her, and headed towards the woods. There were tracks in the wet earth around the barley.

There was an echo screaming back from the woods. 'Come up! Come up, ye hoor!' I went on shouting, becoming detached from myself at the sound of my own voice, and almost forgot the mare I was looking for.

The rotten green fence was pushed over between the field and the woods, where it went into the bottom covert, and her tracks, double-depth with pregnancy, crossed the ditch and carried on through the she-briars and the rancid scattering of last year's leaves. The old bitch was up ahead, lying down in a patch of bluebell leaves; wallowing in the faded flowers. She was chewing on what I prayed was a poisonous plant.

But it was only a dandelion. She stopped chewing and fixed me with a neurotic stare and flapped her lower lip, dripping green-stained froth. She groaned loudly to remind me of her condition and avert retribution.

I stole up to her, calling her dreadful names in a crooning voice. The air was full of the sound of water dripping through the canopy of new leaves. I wasted ten minutes getting the halter on her and persuading her to stand up and come quietly and not miscarry on the way. She jibbed and shied and skittered, and snapped at me. She knew better than to bite, because I would bite back. I had before now.

As we came out of the fringe of leaves at the edge of the wood, it became apparent that something had changed. The world was a different place from the one I had left a quarter of an hour before. The filthy greyness had been wiped from the sky, and it was now an unbearable blue. Behind us, the trees still dripped, but ahead the steam was already rising off the land.

'Summer's come,' I said. But Clytemnestra was too busy shying away from the corpse of a crow that hung on the fence.

The sun was good, and there was heat in it. Day after day it increased into a heatwave and the memory of a cold climate was stripped away. I can't remember anything about school that month, perhaps because it was so intolerable to be in school in that weather that I have erased the memory. Perhaps I didn't go into school much. I was supposed to be studying for the exams, but all my time at home was spent out working in summer clothes. We saved early hay and our skin turned brown, and the strong light bleached my hair to new extremes of whiteness.

Gerard came home, and had us all drinking something that was made with Guinness and ice-cream, which apparently was the done thing among his brightly coloured friends in Dublin. His pigtail was still orange, but the rest of his hair had had highlights bleached into it, which didn't suit him at all. He wore huge black trousers, built for a man twice his stature, held up by a bandolier complete with shells, which he claimed were live. He wore those trousers all the time, even in the hottest weather when he was wilting with the heat. My father was deeply embarrassed by him, but saying less and less, and spending more time sitting by himself in his office. You couldn't count my father's grey hairs any more, and when we stood together I felt that I was towering over him. But I didn't know if I had grown or he had shrunk.

The heat became sultry, and Clytemnestra's teats waxed too soon and set Dervla in a panic, and the mare had to be kept on the front lawn where she could be watched more closely.

On the Saturday evening Mary Howlin and Smallgods Temple came to supper and we ate it in the dining-room. Dervla was mobile enough by then to cook properly. She claimed that she could find nothing in her kitchen, but I think she was hurt that we had managed so well while she was incapacitated. Mary took a great interest in Smallgods, and told him that he would have to come and help her with her young horses. He gave her the impression that he knew everything there was to know about breaking and schooling, which seemed odd to me since he didn't have a horse himself.

I hardly got to say a word to anyone, because of having to jump up every five minutes to stand at the french windows and see what the mare was doing. Delivery was imminent. That was why Mary was there, and even Smallgods had only been asked along as an extra pair of hands.

From my post at the window I was the first to see the flashes of lightning. The old dog came shooting in past me, because it was terrified of thunderstorms. The bang of thunder that followed was almost immediate. The storm had broken directly over our heads. And then the rain fell in a solid sheet of water.

Mary's voice called out behind me, 'Is that mare all right?'

And then she was standing behind me, poking her finger in the small of my back. 'She won't be far wrong,' she said. 'That mare has foals like a cow shitting.'

This time the old cow seemed a bit constipated and by the end of the evening the whole supper table, with the exception of my father, who had gone to bed early, was out on the lawn, holding torches steady and pulling on ropes, and trying to make instructions clear above the noise of the rain, but without shouting in case it would upset the mare.

Dervla's foot was in a black polythene bag so the plaster wouldn't get wet. She was in one of my father's greatcoats, of which, it seemed, she would have fitted into a sleeve, plaster of Paris and all, and perched on a very shaky shooting stick that hadn't been used since one of her relations went to Ascot before the war. She was shining the biggest torch downwards, pointing towards the tiny pair of plastic foal's feet and the hands of the people who heaved on them. Mary Howlin was at the mare's head with a glass of whisky still in her left hand. As fast as she drank it, the whisky was diluted with rain back to the same level.

With the heat of the night those of us on the pulling end wore no coats, and the shirts were stuck to our backs and the hair to our faces, and the curses we muttered were stuck in the air, unheard in the noise of the storm.

The mare heaved with the lightning flashes, and, just as I was convinced that we wouldn't get anywhere, the work was done and a black wet carcass shot out on to the grass, and the three of us landed on our arses in the mud.

Mary Howlin had no time for that sort of clumsiness. She handed me her glass, now filled with water, and she knelt by the foal, thumping and fiddling with it and blowing alcoholic fumes down its throat in a great effort to make it breathe.

In another flash of lightning, I saw Smallgods pick something up off the grass and put it in his pocket, with some trouble because his trousers were so wet. Above the rain, Mary yelled to Dervla that it was a colt, and Dervla was so excited that she lost her balance, and the shooting stick snapped, and she too was arse on the grass beside us.

We laughed, but it was more with relief because the foal was all right, and, although Smallgods was laughing, when I turned the torch on his face I could see that he was watching the foal and thinking of something else. I knew what he had put in his pocket. While a foal is a foetus, something called a hippomane can accumulate in its mouth. This forms a leathery pad which is ejected at birth. If you can find the hippomane and keep it about you, then that foal will always know you and come to you when you want it.

The foal was put to Clytemnestra's head, and I was told to go and get some chilled water, and take my saturated aunt with me. So I heaved her up on her one good foot and bent myself double to get my neck down to the level of her armpit and we hobbled three-legged around the laurels.

Looking up to see the way ahead, I saw the house in silhouette, and the last decrepid macrocarpa towering over the chimneys. There had been a whole row of them once, to shield us from the wind, but only one remained. Dervla said something that was drowned in the rattle of spent thunder, and I stopped to ask her what it was.

'Orestes,' she said. 'Orestes.'

I was about to say that wasn't it time we started giving our horses normal names, but as I looked towards her face there was the biggest flash of light of all, and in the light her face changed from disgruntled wetness to sheer terror, and she let out a scream at the same time as there was a churning roar, and I had to turn my head back towards the house, despite not wanting to.

The macrocarpa was blazing with a fierce yellow fire and toppling through the roof of the house down towards us.

I stood and wondered if we were far enough away from it and whether we were going to be killed, and I watched with a fascination as the weight of the tree sliced our house in half, and I listened to the tearing sound of bricks being pulled apart, and hardly felt Dervla pull on my arm as she threw herself down on the grass, but I wouldn't follow her because I thought that if I was to be killed I wanted to watch it and see how it felt.

And so, the summer began.

I ended up at Ballynell at five in the morning. Mary Howlin gave a bed to the others, but Smallgods brought me back beneath the craggy oak trees where the roosting bantams were rousing themselves for the day ahead. He led me through the peeling kitchen and in and out of dusty rooms to a tiled hall and a groaning staircase. We crept past the rooms where his family slept, and then he stopped and asked me if I wanted a bath. After all the stealth, the normality of his voice was frightening.

I shook my head. 'It's a bit late.' I couldn't imagine a bath at that hour of the morning, but when he asked if I was sure I looked down at myself and saw how dirty I was, and said I wouldn't say no.

He left me in a half-dark room with two beds in it, and there was a loud rush of bathwater, and then I was sinking into the heat of the bath, while Smallgods hovered backwards and forwards carrying towels, and sheets to make my bed with, and apologising for the water not being hot enough, no matter how much I insisted that it was.

He put me into someone else's pyjamas that had no drawstring, and into a starchy bed. I said, 'Is the other bed yours?'

'No,' he said. 'This room is spare.'

There must have been something about the way I asked it, because he sensed that I was appealing to him not to be left alone. He said nothing, but instead of going to his own room he fetched more sheets and made up the bed that was two-foot-six away from me. Once I was certain I wouldn't be on my own, I could allow myself to think that I was exhausted, numb and concave. It must have been after he thought I was asleep that I heard him whispering in the dark. One prayer and then another. I wouldn't ever have thought that Smallgods Temple prayed. I tried to imagine how he might be phrasing it; whether he was as arrogant with God as he was with the rest of us; did he speak to God as an inferior, or was he prepared to acknowledge that he might have one, private, equal?

I was going to say good-night, but I thought he might not thank me if he knew that I had heard him whispering, so I let him think I was asleep, while creatures pattered in the attic above us and slivers of daylight came through the curtains.

Before I could sleep, I had to visualise the house coming down. In that re-enactment I had lost my fascination for the violence of it, and the colours of the blaze. Instead I worried about my father, lying in his bed wtih the ceiling caving in on him. In the real event I had forgotten him completely, until a lightning flash showed our bathroom, the wall collapsed and the bath hanging in mid-air suspended by copper pipes, and my father, still sitting on the lavatory with his eyes staring down at us, and his mouth opened as if he was going to speak.

For the last time in a long time, I cried before I slept.

JUNE

Mrs Temple drove me back to Roscarmony that afternoon. After interrogation by the Deadlies, the wrecking of our house had acquired an anecdotal quality. They had laughed when I told them about my father astride the lavatory in the lightning, and made me repeat it with more details until it ceased to be a nightmare and became a funny story.

The damage was not as bad as it had seemed in the dark; only the end wall of the house was missing. Dervla was swinging around the ruins on her crutches. As the van drew up she came towards us.

'It was very kind of you,' she began to say, and then Mrs Temple said, 'Dervla?' as if she recognised my aunt, but wasn't sure.

'Franny?' Dervla said, in the same tone. 'God, of course. Temple. I thought I knew the name. So you married him? Everyone said you would.'

Mrs Temple threw a nervous glance at me, and Dervla took her meaning, and said, 'Well, how are you? God, it's years since I saw you. You're looking great. I wish I'd known you were living so close. All this time.'

It turned out they had known each other at Trinity, seventeen years before. When they had gone through all the sentences that long-lost acquaintances have for each other, and discussed the damage to the house, Mrs Temple offered to have me to stay.

'He'd be no trouble. Godfrey and I talked about it this morning. With the exams coming up next week, we thought the best thing would be if he stayed until they were over. He and Smallgods can do their studying together.'

'It's very kind,' Dervla said. 'It's up to him. Do you want to go?'

'I don't mind,' I said.

'The I-don't-mind-generation,' Dervla said, and she and Mrs Temple laughed.

When she had gone, I turned on Dervla and said, 'That can't be right.'

'What can't?'

'Smallgods is eighteen years old, and if she was at university with you seventeen years ago, and not married?'

'Don't be digging up old scandal,' she said.

'What scandal?' I knew she would have to tell me, in case I asked Smallgods about it.

'I'll tell you if you promise not to be talking about it. It was a long time ago, and as likely as not your friend Smallgods doesn't know about it himself. Franny had a baby while she was at Trinity, and the father was supposed to be an Englishman, who lit out of it as soon as he heard she was pregnant. Anyway, she was fairly amazing about it, considering the times that were in it, and how young she was. She was very headstrong. She said she was going to keep the baby and bring it up herself. Godfrey Temple was the brother of the father of the child. He was some sort of Gaeilgeoir poet, and he stood by her and the child was named after him. The last I heard she was going to marry him.'

'So Smallgods' father is his uncle? That's a bit of a coincidence.'

'What is?'

'Him being brought up by his uncle and me being brought up by my aunt.'

'It's not a coincidence at all,' she said. 'Don't talk rubbish.'

And then we had to turn towards the house, and wonder what to do with it.

'How's the foal?' I said.

'The foal is fine, I think. The mare won't let me near it.'

Life at Ballynell was fairly easy, so long as you kept out of Oldgods' way and remembered not to speak English in his presence. I forgot sometimes, and the room would fall into silence. But because I was a visitor I got away with a glare. I didn't know what the punishment would have been for the rest of them, because they kept to the rules. Most of the time I had no idea what was being talked about, because my Irish wasn't up to it.

Mrs Temple tried to put the bright side to me. 'You should do well in your Irish-exam orals after all this.' I didn't have the heart to tell her that I had become more confused than ever about the language.

The mystery of Smallgods' sandwiches was explained. They were so poor that most mornings there was only pink baloney sausage to make sandwiches with, and Smallgods either contrived to leave them at home, or put them in the dustbin as soon as he reached school. He said that one should only eat food if it was a pleasure, and that most people ate more than was good for them in any case. The smoked salmon and game that he had from time to time were presents from their better-off relations. After the first day I was starving to death, so I used to take him down the town at lunchtime for a feed of fish and chips. He said that he had never eaten fish and chips before, but I couldn't believe that. Sometimes he went a bit too far.

Mrs Temple would go to bed, racked and ashen, before nine every evening. She collapsed into a chair before the television at about seven, and dozed while one of her daughters brushed her hair. She would seem to be asleep, but if the brushing stopped she woke, and said, 'Don't stop. Not yet.'

Smallgods and I studied in the unused drawing-room among sagging furniture. There was never a fire, but a black mass of stuff stuck to the grate.

'What's that?' I said.

'That was last Christmas,' he said. 'We ran out of fuel, and mother tried to burn her old records to get a fire going. Of course, they only melted. I told her they would. Glen Miller and Roy Orbison. We ended up burning an armchair in the sitting-room fire.'

Smallgods was reading Aeschylus out loud, for my benefit. He said if we were going to give the horses those names I might as well know the whole story. He screeched at all the screechy bits and asked me why Dervla had never called a horse Cassandra. I was trying to understand mathematical theorems, but I might as well have been trying to get milk from a bull.

'I've applied for art,' he said.

'What?'

'I'm going to be a painter. I've applied to do art at Limerick. They will have me if I get a pass in the exam.'

'Do you think you'll pass?' I said.

He sneered. 'A monkey could pass those exams.'

'I mightn't.'

'I'll tell you what,' he said. 'We'll go for a bit of a walk.'

Those midnight walks by the river became a habit. He would stride through the fields as though he could see in the dark, and we would talk about getting boats to row backwards and forwards between Ballynell and Roscarmony. Sometimes I tried asking him leading questions to see if he knew anything about his illegitimate origins, but as far as I could tell he was unaware of any of it.

'You should come to Italy with us,' he said. 'In August. To stay with my uncle. You can't know anything about pleasure until you know Italy.'

'We'll be too busy,' I said. 'On the farm.'

When the exams were over, and I was back at home being a farmer from dawn to dusk, I said to my father, 'Smallgods asked me out to Italy for August.'

'That's a pity,' he said. 'It would have been nice for you to go.'

'I thought,' I said, 'I thought you wouldn't miss me for a week or two.'

My father looked old. Every day he looked a week older and some days he looked a month younger.

'Whatever you think,' he said. 'Everyone needs a holiday.'

I thought Dervla might object, but she said that we all needed to get away. She looked as though she might be crying, but I couldn't tell, because I had never seen her crying before.

'I nearly went to Italy once,' she said, but she wouldn't say any more.

JULY

There was no time to think in July. When I wasn't working on the farm I was helping the builders, who had nearly finished the remaking of our house. My father and I slept down the other end, in Gerard's room, beneath the posters of punk rockers and the nihilistic slogans of his generation. I offered to take them down, but he said, 'No, *a ghrá*. Gerard will want them when he gets his room back. Leave them up. I don't see them anyway.'

Smallgods came over nearly every day. I was surprised to see that he would do physical labour, and within a week he spoke as though he knew more about farming than I did. As he was working for us anyway, my father offered him a job, and he accepted it. It meant that he had to get up at six to bicycle to Roscarmony by eight. Sometimes he rode Dervla's horse, and he rode it with a sort of neatness that made me feel like a cowboy on mine. On Sundays we went show-jumping at the small gymkhanas. He was fiercely competitive, and sulked if he didn't get a clear round. We used to stand by the ring, waiting our turn, with our legs forward over the front of the saddles, tapping our whips on the flaps and talking. Dervla would hobble between us and the car, trying to make us eat sausage rolls and telling us the breeding of all the other horses.

He charmed Clytemnestra into letting him handle her foal, and he soon had the foal so tame that it would come when he called it. He said, 'I'll buy this foal from you one of the days. It will be the right age when I've left art school and am making a fortune.'

'The best artists died in poverty,' I said.

He said, 'David Hockney does all right. I have no intention of being the best artist, only the wealthiest one. It is all a question of hype.'

'Good for you,' I said. I asked him where he was going to stay in Limerick, and that made him laugh.

'With a priest,' he said. 'Oldgods has arranged for me to stay with a Gaeilgeoir priest friend of his until I can find a flat. But he isn't bad, this priest. A bit peculiar, but not bad.'

For the first time I had a twinge of envy. I was only getting a year at the local agricultural college, while Smallgods was in for four years of Bohemia, even if he did have to begin it living with a priest. He didn't say so, but he was hoarding all the money he earned on the farm, knowing that it would be all he had to stretch his grant.

He took me to a concert in Waterford, and taught me to pogo. Pogoing was way out of fashion by then. The rest of the audience were New Romantic posers who could barely dance at all. But Smallgods and I spent the evening springing up and down on the spot, until a bouncer came over and said, 'That's enough of that.'

'What on earth do you mean?' Smallgods said in his most superior voice. But in the noise of the music it was lost on the bouncer, and we were thrown out of the hall anyway.

Then the plans were laid for Busto Arsizio. Normally, Oldgods flew ahead on his own and left his wife to drive the children down through France. I couldn't understand, if they were so poor, how they could afford to get there, but it was taken care of somehow. I suspected that the uncle might have paid, but I could have been wrong. Smallgods said that there would be a crush in the car, and he was all for the two of us hitching down, as he had done in the spring. I knew if I said that to Dervla she would insist on paying for an air fare, leaving Smallgods to hitch on his own, so I pretended to her that it was all taken care of, and in the evening I would get out a map of France and try to imagine what the towns looked like. Smallgods gave me *Le Grand Meaulnes* to read, and then I thought that France must be a place full of tiny roads and wedding feasts in decaying manors. A bit like Wexford but colder.

AUGUST

Leaving Ireland for the first time was an act of courage. Although the sea was calm I was sick from nervousness. France turned out to be nothing but a blur of autoroutes with Smallgods chattering in French to the lorry drivers. We stopped in one small town because Smallgods said he had to go to a pâtisserie. The cakes were nice enough, I suppose, but I couldn't see what the fuss was about. I asked him why there were three horse's heads over one of the shops, and he told me that it was because they sold horsemeat. After that I couldn't pass through France quickly enough.

Italy was better. From the way Smallgods had talked about it I was expecting paradise, and my other preconceptions about it were entirely mythical. Horatius and Buonarroti, and Forster heroines in long white dresses. To arrive in a place and be told that you are in heaven is difficult.

Once we had crossed the mountains there were long straight roads that led nowhere, lined with desecrated stumps of trees, and surrounded by a landscape that looked too cultivated to be beautiful, and seemed almost deserted.

'Italy is an urban society,' he said. 'Their greatest fear is being alone, so they crowd together in the cities and live for pleasure.'

'Do they eat horses?' I said.

He didn't answer, only clicked his tongue at me and looked at me as if I was stupid. I took it to mean that they did eat horses.

I was perpetually losing my sense of direction, and the

middles of the days were amputated by a hotness that you couldn't breathe in. Everyone seemed to be either arguing ferociously, or throwing their arms around each other. Old people would mistake me for a German because of my hair, and refuse to serve me in the shops, until Smallgods explained to them that I was Irish, when they became as effusive and friendly as they had been hateful in the beginning. Not that there were many shops open. In August everything closed at the same time while the whole population went on holiday together, so as not to be lonely, I suppose.

The Temple house was the largest in a small village called Madelfino Ardoltinezzi, north of Busto Arsizio. It was the strangest house I had ever been in, with the lower rooms more like stables, converted into bathrooms and storerooms and a kitchen, all with bars on the windows. Living was carried on on the upper floors, where all the windows had balconies with flowers dripping down from them, and the furniture was made from leather and stainless steel. I was expecting to meet the uncle who owned the house, but I was told that he always went away when Smallgods' family came. When I heard that, I knew he must be the one who was Smallgods' father.

The chief inhabitant of the village was a man called Fabio Arnolfini, who was one of those architect-designers of immense fame and indefinable wealth who exist only in Italy. He lived in the yellow house next door, the inside of which made the Temples' house seem normal. But if Fabio's house was a nightmare, it was nothing compared to his garden, which was a monstrous concoction of five acres, full of parrots and weird statues, and hedges clipped into unnatural shapes by a team of snarling, half-naked gardeners. Smallgods said that the Temples' house was only Corb. while Fabio's was pure Memphis, but at the time those expressions meant nothing to me. The one good thing about Fabio's garden was an Olympic-sized swimming pool (decorated with Formica knobs), which we spent most of the days in, or around. Fabio lived on his own. I was told that his wife didn't talk to him, and lived in Milan.

I began to like Italy on about the third morning, when I was woken after a night of heat by Smallgods with my breakfast. It was black coffee and ice-cream, and while I ate it, half asleep, with Smallgods laughing at me, I began to realise, for the first time, the pleasure of eating.

Perhaps that was not disconnected from another discovery of a pleasure I had made the night before. Since the incident with Sarah by the river, I had had one or two attempts at self-abuse, with no success. Perhaps my technique had lacked something, or perhaps it was the cold of the bathroom tiles on my feet, but it wasn't until the heat of the Italian night, sleeping in a room to myself for the first time, that I worked out the correct manipulatory procedure. I was expecting guilt, but all I got afterwards was a good night's sleep.

Everything seemed right for the rest of that day. Even the pollarded trees took on a sort of manipulated beauty. While we were by the pool, Fabio came down to see us with a monkey on his shoulder, and I said to him, 'That's what I love about Italians. They aren't afraid to give children names that mean fabulous.'

Fabio hadn't a clue what I was saying, until Smallgods caught on and snorted with laughter, and said, 'Fabulous is *favoloso*. Fabio is a kind of bean.'

Fabio began to speak to me with great attention. He swatted a fly from my bare shoulder and asked me if I had a girlfriend.

'Fabio, don't,' Smallgods said. 'Not him.'

He said it with such authority that Fabio sulked and marched away, talking to his monkey in Italian.

'What was all that about?' I said.

'Nothing,' Smallgods said. 'He's very nice really. You just have to watch him from time to time. And if he asks you again, invent a girlfriend.'

I don't know why the nightmares started, but the more I

enjoyed the days in Italy, the worse the nightmares became. Smallgods would rush in from his room next door and wake me up, because he said that I was screaming and would rouse the rest of the household. I would be covered in sweat, whether from the heat or fear, I don't know.

I told him I was afraid of losing my mind.

'Why?' he said.

And then I told him about my mother. I had never told anyone about her before, except Sarah, and she had dragged it out of me. Smallgods just sat on the bed and listened. I told him about the time she had come home from the asylum, and we were told that she was our mother. Even Gerard, who could remember her, couldn't recognise her. We were afraid and hid from her, and I wouldn't come out from behind Dervla's legs if my mother was in the room. So she screamed at us and smashed everything in the house, and she was taken away again. She might have got better – she might never have died – if we, her own children, had been nicer to her.

'No,' he said. 'You can't blame yourself for something like that.'

'She killed herself,' I said. 'I don't know for sure, but I think she did. And when I was told about it, it meant nothing at all.'

'It does now,' he said.

'It's too late.'

He said nothing, but held me by the wrist. I wondered if he was reassuring himself more than he was reassuring me.

'Am I mad?' I said.

'I don't know. You are very different. But there's no harm in that. I wouldn't like you if you were not.'

THE SECOND YEAR

SEPTEMBER

Morning came to one of those bottomless nights and Elsa Ponder crept into the half-shuttered room. She was shoeless and silent, with her hair tied back, and smiling quietly to herself as she sat on the bed. She put her hand across the mound beneath the bedclothes and leaned towards the breathing face, and let her other hand trace the stray bit of hair that curled over his ear.

Smallgods woke, without opening his eyes. He said good morning to her without a sound, by moving his mouth only, dry with the long hours of sleeping, and then he smiled at the touch of her finger on his cheek.

'Is it you?' he said.

'Hardly the Holy Father,' she said.

She whispered something in his ear and made him laugh until she kissed him. 'I shouldn't be doing that,' she said.

His arms bound to his sides by her weight on the counterpane, he kept his eyes closed and his face still while her tongue crept around his lips, and then he opened his mouth wide, and let her count his teeth, one by one.

It was minutes before she stood up, telling him to get out of the bed and not waste the whole morning when he should be at school. The light caught her face as he opened his eyes. It was not a beautiful face by any conventional standard. Her nose was spherical and her teeth were short, like milk teeth. She had too much of the child about her for beauty, but her childishness was only apparent in a state of happiness. At other times she could look old with worry, beyond the menopause.

His arms free, he stretched them over his head, and said that he wouldn't get up, and she fell down again on top of him, and ran her fingers through his armpits.

'Don't be revolting,' he said, smelling the scent she had raised.

She said, 'I like it.' And she pushed her hands on, over the flesh of his back and up to the nape of his neck, where she clutched the hair in her fingers. She put her chin into his collarbone and ground it in the hollow above, and pushed her hips against the bedclothes.

'If this goes on,' he said, 'I won't be able to help myself. I'm sure your mother told you one thing leads to another.'

'Get up, so,' she said, pulling on the blankets as she stood. He pulled back, until she pulled him out of bed and he spilled on to the floor in a tangle of blanket and skin, and tried to pull her down to him.

'No,' she said. 'Get up.'

She pecked him on the nose, and told him that he should be ashamed of himself to be rolling on the floor without a stitch. He wrapped a sheet around himself with mock modesty and headed towards the bathroom.

She sat on the side of the shower, with her sleeve rolled up, running her fingers between his toes.

'Where's your modesty now?' he said. 'Look at the state you have me in.' But she wouldn't look up, so he told her that she was getting wet, and tried to concentrate on washing. Then, in a voice that wasn't her own, she asked him if he loved her.

He couldn't think of any answer except that he did, and, telling her again that she was getting wet, he turned his head into the heat of the water to wash away the lie. She smiled her relief into the back of his knee and held her hand out into the spatter of water.

She said suddenly and in a loud voice, 'Oh God. I'll never get me work done. Father Mulrahey will eat me alive. And will you look at me, I'm soaked to the skin.' She stood and gave him a loud smack on the backside, and when she got to the door she half turned back. 'Father Mulrahey is out anointing a poor woman with a tumor on the brain and three pregnant daughters. He won't be back until twelve. I'd better go and see to your bed for you; the way you won't be held up doing it on your way to school.'

She went back to the bedroom, and tidied it, and made the bed, and undressing to her underwear, got into it. She lay there worrying until he came back into the room, when she found that a smile cracked across her face at the surprise on his.

When he put his head between her legs, he heard a sob and, looking up, saw an expression that was something like weeping.

'Sorry,' he said. 'Don't you like that?'

'No, it isn't that. It's nice. It's just no one ever had that kind of consideration for me before.'

'You married women are all the same.' He said it to make her laugh, and it did.

'Much you'd know,' she said '*Garsún.*'

She laughed so that her breastless nipples shook, like two wild strawberries on her white skin, and then a moment later her face was serious again as he bent his head between her thighs.

Father Damon Mulrahey was the Curate of Tinnahinchy, five miles out of Limerick, past Ballinacurra and the Regional and the Crescent, and on towards Tralee, but away to the left off the main road. Tinnahinchy was a village with fifteen houses, three of them public, and one that used to be a shop. The priest's house was a tall house, alone at the edge of the village, by the church. It looked as though it had been transplanted whole from an old suburban terrace and set in a half-acre of clover and rhododendron. The stairs sagged in the middles of the steps, and each one creaked in a different tone as you ascended, so that if Smallgods came back in the small hours of the morning he had to sit on the banisters and haul himself up to avoid waking the priest. It was the sort of house where a small noise echoed from one end to the other, and even the mice had learned the art of silence.

Elsa Ponder came in every day to cook and clean. Her mother had been the housekeeper until the arthritis got her. Jack Ponder, Elsa's husband, had taken advantage of the high unemployment in the area, and sat at home, half a mile away, watching racehorses on the television. When Elsa had cooked the priest's dinner, she would return to cook his, and then bicycle back to the village to make the priest his tea. She had married young, for her own good reasons, and had never fallen victim to love until the arrival of Smallgods Temple. For three weeks she had tried to communicate her love to him, making stealthy progress in intimacy and flirtation, until the morning she had found him in his bed and pulled him out of it, hoping to see his naked body on the floor. It was the sight of his skin, still tinted with brown from Italy, that decided her. But the force of her decision, and the strength of her longing for his skin, frightened her. She held back, and then followed him to the shower. She had to justify her decision first. She had never intended to ask him if he loved her. She heard the question at the same time as he heard it. When he answered that he did, she was so frightened that she wanted to run out of the house. But a wave of bravado came over her, and she heard herself challenging him to sleep with her. He was the third man she had known. The first was her father, and the second was her husband, and both of them were blurred into the same horror. She lay in his bed waiting for him, with her fingers and legs crossed for luck. She reassured herself with the thought that the third was always lucky. She thought, at the age of twenty-two, that it was time she did something for her own pleasure, and not the appeasement of someone else. For the first few minutes, when he had slipped into bed with her, she couldn't stop shaking, and she couldn't stop touching his skin. He thought that she was cold, and pulled the covers close around them, and rubbed her back to warm her.

Afterwards, he sat rigid like a statue at Luxor, with his back to the headboard, and fingered her hair. It was brown, and so fine that, one by one, the strands were invisible. She chewed on his thumb with her short teeth.

She said. 'You have three hairs on your chest. You'll have more when you're older.'

He said, 'I suppose I had to lose it some time.'

'What did you lose?'

He laughed at her. 'When I'm famous you'll be able to sell your story to the papers, as the woman who stole my innocence. A life of debauchery starts here.'

'Much you know about debauchery,' she said.

There was barely time to dress and put the dinner on before the priest came back. She was flustered as she rushed in and out of the kitchen, serving the two men their meal. And she was convinced that the priest would guess what was going on from the looks that Smallgods gave her whenever she entered the dining-room. She made mistakes: burned the cabbage; spilled the soup. 'I'm sorry, Father. I'm a bit behind. I didn't get in 'till late this morning.'

'Nothing wrong at home, I hope?'

She couldn't think of a second lie to build on the first one, but fortunately the priest was paying more attention to Smallgods.

'No school today, Godfrey?'

She envied the casualness with which Smallgods could lie. He said that one of his tutors was sick, and he had decided to stay home and get on with a project.

Father Mulrahey was a massive man, with black hair pouring out of his collar and cuffs. In his black uniform he looked like a buffalo. But he handled his knife and fork with a comical delicacy, making courteous gestures in the air as he talked. If his voice seemed affected, it was only perhaps that he was trying to modulate it to be less harsh than it was by nature. He shaved three times a day, and clipped the excess hair from his eyebrows and nose in his battle to be less of a beast and more of a human.

To Elsa's horror, when she came to clear the plates away, they seemed to be discussing adultery.

'Do you really believe that?' Smallgods was saying. 'Apart from being a priest, do you believe that?'

'I am nothing apart. There is no conflict between being a priest and being myself. I believe that.'

'So all sinful love is a perversion? All love that is unsanctified by the Church is a sickness of the soul? How can the love of an atheist be a sickness, and exactly the same love in a Catholic be ordained by God? How can adultery not be love, if it is felt and expressed in exactly the same way as love in a marriage? And can the love within a marriage be, as you claim, basically the same sort of love as the love of a child, or the love of God? Does a priest fancy his flock?'

Instead of being angered by Smallgods' taunt, the priest smiled at him indulgently. 'Dear boy,' he said. 'You are very young. Pure love, as Our Lord has shown us, is chaste. The other manifestations of what you call love are given to us for the procreation of children. To abuse them is to abuse a gift from God.'

The last thing Elsa heard as she left the room was Smallgods laughing, and saying, 'Sounds a bit like sour grapes to me.'

When she reached the safety of the other side of the door, she thought that her legs would give way beneath her. She had never imagined that anyone would speak to a priest like that. She had been brought up to believe that if you insulted a priest you would be turned to stone on the spot. And she couldn't understand why Father Mulrahey was being so indulgent. Why, instead of being angry, he was smiling at Smallgods all the time.

'The man must be a saint,' she thought.

And then she was angry with Smallgods, for risking their

secret. She realised then that Smallgods had nothing to lose by what they had done. If a life was to be destroyed it would be hers. She was still angry when she returned with their coffee and biscuits.

'I have to go now,' she said. 'I'll wash the dishes this afternoon.'

She wouldn't look at Smallgods, although she could sense him trying to catch her eye. The priest seemed surprised by the tone in her voice, and when his eye rested on her she felt as though she was naked, and he could see her sin.

There was a strong wind as she cycled home, so that when she arrived it seemed as though her eyes were watering from that.

She was nervous in front of Jack, afraid that he might notice something. He ate his dinner without taking his eyes from the television, as usual, but when he had finished he narrowed his eyes and said, 'You're very jumpy today.'

She said nothing, but she knew from the tone of his voice what was coming next. He always wanted to do it when she was upset. As if her weakness turned him on in some way.

'Come into the bedroom for a minute,' he said.

She followed him out of a habit of obedience, and stood feeling helpless as he removed his shirt and lay back on the bed with his right hand thrust down the front of his trousers.

'No,' she said. 'Not now. It's the middle of the day. Anyone could call to the door.'

His hand was moving in his trousers, as if he was taking pleasure in the revulsion on her face. He propped himself up on his elbow, and cajoled her.

'Elsa. Come over here to me.'

She took a step towards him, and he smiled, but then she changed course and went across to the other side of the room where she opened a drawer and began to rummage in it, as if she was looking for something.

'Ah now,' he said.

And then he was standing behind her with his hard arms around her ribcage, pushing himself into her backside, whispering into her ear that she could come to bed for a minute or two, and he knew it wasn't important to her, but it meant a lot to him, and the Lord knew he loved her. His voice had a ring of sincerity, but she had heard the same words in the same tone before, from him, and from her father before him, so she tried to pretend that he wasn't there, and went on sorting through the drawer, while he went on stroking her chest. But every stroke of his fingers was like the stroke of a truncheon, and his voice went through her head like fingernails on slate.

Then the image of Smallgods tangled in the blankets came into her mind, and she knew that something had changed in her. Having done something once for her own pleasure, she had annexed her own body for the first time, and there was no going back. With as much strength as she had, she drew her elbow forward and gave him a blow in the ribs that sent him reeling across the room, and at the same time she shouted at him.

'Oh fuck off, Jack Ponder.'

She came to Smallgods while the priest was saying late Mass on Sunday. She had planned it, and made a shepherd's pie the day before so that there was nothing to cook on Sunday morning. Smallgods had a bottle of Cointreau, and he made her kiss him while his mouth was full of it. She was reluctant; she said that Jack would smell it on her breath, but then she believed him when he said that Jack wouldn't know what the smell of Cointreau was.

'It's a celebration,' he said. 'I found a flat. In Mallow Street. John Donahugh is going to America for three months, so I have it free until Christmas if I water his plants.'

She felt as though someone had dropped a weight on her.

'Oh God,' she said.

'What?'

'You're leaving. What will I do?'

He winced, and prised her fingers from his shoulder as if they were tentacles. 'What's that got to do with it? This was a temporary arrangement. I can't live with a priest for the rest of my life.'

He thought she was going to cry, so he said, 'It's only in Limerick. Five miles, for God's sake. You go into Limerick twice a week as it is.'

She picked up the bottle as if she was going to take a drink from it, but instead she shook it, and said, 'Was this full? It's nearly empty. You must be drunk.'

'I'd better finish it, so,' he said, and she handed him the bottle. He drained it in a single draught. She put her head on his chest, and when she looked up again he was asleep. She picked up his wrist and looked at his watch, and saw that she would be safe for another three or four minutes. She didn't want to leave him until the very last moment. She settled him into a more comfortable position, with his head on her lap, and his sleep was so deep and drugged that she could do it without waking him. She found that she was feeling fidgety, and she began to make his hair into small plaits to occupy her hands, thinking that she could undo them before she left.

She had decided not to think, and that took so much concentration that she forgot about the time. The sound of the front door slamming brought her to her senses, and she jumped to her feet, grabbing her clothes and a handful of Kleenex. When she was half dressed, she heard the ascending creaks of the stairs and hid behind the door, hardly able to button herself, her fingers were shaking so much. She begged St Jude to send the priest to the lavatory first; for his bladder to be full, so that he would walk straight past the door and not look in.

When she heard the lavatory door shut, there was no time to stop and think, or thank St Jude. She flew across the landing with her shoes in her hand and leapt on to the banisters, sliding down them at a speed that made her think she would be killed at the bottom. She landed in the hall without a sound, and escaped the back way, stopping only to put the shepherd's pie in the oven.

She need not have rushed. Father Mulrahey was concentrating on his second pogonotomous act of the day. He was humming as the razor scraped. Saying Mass always raised his spirits. It was the only part of his job that really appealed to him. He tried to make his congregation laugh in the middle of his sermons so that they were on his side when he came to the raising of the Host. At that part of the ceremony, he intoned the words like a Shakespearian actor, believing that the rows of people in front of him were as caught up in the drama as he was.

Newly mown, Father Mulrahey came out of the bathroom and, hearing snores, stopped at Smallgods' door. If you were noticing that sort of thing, you would have said that he stopped and looked at the sleeping figure a little longer than was necessary.

Then he bellowed, 'Godfrey! Wake up! Lunchtime!'

Smallgods stirred and opened one dead eye and said, 'Yes.'

'I thought I didn't see you at Mass. You young people sleep too much.'

Father Mulrahey went down and took the shepherd's pie from the oven, and put it on the table that was already laid, and sat in front of it, waiting for Smallgods.

He was a long time in coming, and he had a green tinge to his face. When he sat down, Father Mulrahey began to spoon the pie on to the plates.

'This food seems very cold. There must be something wrong with that oven.'

Inexplicably, Smallgods said, 'God is a man, and he's laughing.'

'Laughing at whom?'

'Women. Mostly. Anyone he can get a laugh out of. Creation was a joke. Women are the butt of creation.'

'I don't follow.'

Smallgods was trying not to inhale the smell of the food beneath his nose. His cheeks inflated once, as if he was trying not to be sick. He said, 'Don't you know, Damon? Eunuched by your vows. You never talk about that. Not the man to judge, but there you sat. I mean sit. Has it withered away?'

The priest swivelled to inspect Smallgods closely. He saw the small plaits pointing backwards in the boy's hair, and the way he was swaying, and the rolling eyes.

'Are you feeling sick?'

'I think I'm drunk. I drank some Cointreau. I think I'm going to throw up. Undignified.'

Damon Mulrahey said, 'Perhaps it would be better if you went to the bathroom. Out of consideration for the carpet and Mrs Ponder's workload.'

Smallgods ran away from the table, his cheeks bulging in and out, and the priest readdressed himself to his meal, until it was finished.

When the priest had scraped up the last of his gravy with the last of his brown bread, he got to his feet slowly and went to find the boy. He stopped outside the bathroom, and rapped on the door lightly with his fingers.

'Godfrey?'

He pushed the door open. Smallgods was still hunched over the bowl of the lavatory, with his eyes wide open, staring into it. He couldn't move because of the ache in his head and the weight of his limbs. His hands held tight on to the porcelain and there was a drip of spittle from the corner of his mouth.

Damon put his two hands on the boy's shoulders, and asked him if he was all right, and Smallgods shook his head, as much to shake the loudness of Damon's voice out of it as to say no. Damon bent close over him, and whispered in his ear that he should go back to bed, and sleep it off. Smallgods nodded, and the priest pulled him to his feet and helped him along the corridor, and off with his outer clothes. When he was in the bed, Damon sat on beside him, with one hand on his shoulder, as he often sat on the beds of the sick and dying.

'Damon, you're a true friend. Why are you never angry with me?'

'I don't know,' the priest said. 'I wonder sometimes myself. I think you remind me of someone else I knew once.'

'I could sleep now, Damon. Honestly, I'm all right. I could sleep. You don't have to stay.'

But Damon stayed. His hand was kneading slightly on Smallgods' shoulder. He was saying things, in a stuttering voice, but the pain in Smallgods' head was too great for him to concentrate and decipher them. Smallgods began to drift into sleep, wondering why Damon was stuttering when normally his speech was so fluid.

When Smallgods woke again it was dark. Damon was gone but the pain in his head was still with him. The room was so black and silent that he wondered if he was dead and gone to hell, and then, with the alcohol, the thought of hell made him afraid. He lay, in a state of pure fear, for what he thought was a long time, until he heard the creaks on the stairs, and then he waited, praying that Damon would look in on him.

The door opened inwards and cast a light across the room. There was the smell of shaving foam that Damon carried everywhere with him.

'You're awake. How do you feel now? Are you better? I'll have you join the Pioneers yet.'

'I'm fine. I'm fine now.'

Damon came and sat again on the bed. 'Good. That's good. Get some more sleep. I was just going to bed myself. I brought you a glass of water.'

The priest made to stand up.

'Damon?'

'What?'

'Damon. Will you do me a favour?'

'What?'

'Stay for a bit. Don't leave me on my own?'

'Will I turn the light on? Do you want to talk?'

'No. Don't. Just stay.'

Damon settled himself back against the headboard and lit a cigarette. When he pulled on it you could see the room reflected in his eyes.

Smallgods said, 'I was just afraid, that's all. I never told anyone I was afraid before.'

'Your secret is safe with me.'

'Listen, I'm sorry. I've been lousy to you.'

'Young people are never easy,' Damon said. He pulled Smallgods' head over on to his chest, like a comforter would, and Smallgods drifted in and out of sleep in the glow and darkness of the cigarette. He shifted his arm to make himself more comfortable, and it brushed against the back of Damon's hand. Damon let out something that was almost like a moan, and the skin on the back of his hand was hot. Smallgods could make out his lips moving as if he was saying his prayers.

After sleep, the next thing that Smallgods was aware of was the touch of rough skin against his face. Then he realised that the skin itself wasn't rough. It was stubble. A mouth pressed on his own, with groans of greed and twenty years of deprivation coming from the back of the throat. Smallgods was frozen, while he tried to decide whether it could really be happening, or whether he was still drunk and dreaming.

Involuntarily, Smallgods opened his mouth to gag, and then he knew he was awake. He thought that if he was sick that would solve the problem, but then he realised that his stomach was empty from being sick in the afternoon, and all he did was gag. A huge tongue came pushing into his mouth; a tongue that felt as though it must be three times the size of his own. Smallgods opened his mouth as wide as disgust could make him, and summoned all the fear and anger that was in him, and brought his two sets of teeth crashing together on the wad of purple meat that lay between them. When he bit he held on, while the priest struggled and made noises like a pig squealing in death. He clenched his teeth together, and drank the blood, until the priest subsided, whimpering, on to the floor.

Smallgods Temple took his time dressing. He carefully washed away the blood from his face and chest, and picked out those of his clothes that were neatest, freshly ironed by Elsa. In the kitchen he smoked one of Damon's cigarettes to kill the last of the taste of the blood, while he waited for the morning, or Dr Powers, whichever came first.

OCTOBER

In a small, dishevelled house on King's Island, the sort that is let to art students, Roland de Tiernaux hung upside down, by the tips of his small feet, from the lintel of the kitchen doorway, swaying slightly now and then, but not more than might make you think that there was a bit of a draught between the kitchen and the sitting-room.

The door itself had been missing since the cold winter of '76, when a ceramics student had run out of firewood, and decided that it was surplus to the structural integrity of the building. The stair banisters had met the same fate, but they had been replaced by a subsequent student sculptor, the subject of whose thesis was the phallic relevance of Corinthian columns in eighteenth-century Irish architecture. The door was found to be irreplaceable, partly because there wasn't a carpenter in Limerick as cock-eyed as the original builder of the house, and partly because the house was so small that it was felt that a new door would take up an unnecessary amount of space.

Roland de Tiernaux, whose name was pronounced Dettirnicks, was learning to be a painter. For three years his tutors had done everything in their power to persuade him to paint something that wasn't a Friesian cow, and had failed. He couldn't explain it himself, but every time he put pencil to paper, black-and-white cows appeared. He was from Co. Tipperary, and he went home to the farm every weekend to study the dairy herd. This term he had taken up yoga, Buddhism and ju-jitsu all in the same week, and he liked to spend Monday mornings hanging from the lintel to get himself supple.

He groaned. His face had turned an intense red, and his spectacles were steamed, and his mouth was turned up at the corners in a vaguely masochistic grin. He was a small man, so short that, stretched from the door-lintel, his fingertips swung eleven inches above the ground. The slightness of his stature made you wonder if he was a child with a false beard and a rather strong, grown-up odour. The beard was bright-orange, full of the remains of old brown rice and lentils, and almost as intense in colour as his blood-filled face. The odour was as strong as the smell from a goat, but more human in character. He groaned again, still grinning, and opened his eyes behind the clouded glasses, and rotated his eyeballs, until they came to rest on Jean Spat.

Jean Spat shared the house with him. She sat cross-legged on a three-legged armchair, manipulating wooden knitting needles with which she was knitting thin strands of copper wire, and occasionally, when her attention strayed, her own hair. Now and again she glanced at the clock to see when Roland's hour was up, and a thin macrobiotic hand would leave off the knitting and smooth the copper cloth over shit-green home-dyed trousers.

There was a knock on the front door, so loud that a sheaf of layout papers leapt off the workdesk. Neither of the people moved. There was another knock.

'I wonder who that is?' Roland said.

Jean shrugged her shoulders without leaving off the knitting. If it was someone who knew the way of the house, they would know to push the door open.

Smallgods stood outside in the drizzle, in a long black coat he had found beneath the stairs at Ballynell, waiting for an answer. Finally, he bent down to look through the letterbox, and the door gave way beneath his hand. He pushed it open, knocking over the bicycle on the other side, and let himself in.

Jean made him tea, but it took him half an hour to give the reason for his visit. In the meantime Roland had come down from his lintel. He did it by simply letting go, and landing with a crash on his head on the floor. He was laughing when he stood up.

'You must have a hard head,' Smallgods said.

'Hard enough,' he said, but his response to the question was shifty, as if Smallgods' remark had been too personal for comfort.

'I was going to ask the two of you,' Smallgods said. 'I wondered if it would be all right if I stayed here for a couple of days, until John Donahugh goes to America. I'm a bit stuck.'

'There's only the sofa,' Jean said. 'Do you have a sleeping bag?'

'I'll be fine. The sofa is fine. Thanks,' he said. 'I'll have to go out to Tinnahinchy to collect a few things, but not today.'

On Wednesday afternoon, Smallgods sat at the back of Tinnahinchy church, and watched the priest come out of the vestry and stand by his altar. In the weak light, he was like a pillar of black cloth, with a white face on top of it. Damon stood, and turned his head rather than his eyes, as if his eyes were fixed in their sockets. His face was framed with blue hair and the blue shadow on his chin, and he turned once to each of the darkest spaces in the church, as though he knew that someone was there.

He didn't know yet if he had preached his last sermon, or what happened to priests once the power of speech had left them. Seeing a figure in the back row, and seeing that it was Smallgods, a greeting came out of his throat by instinct, but as it reached his mouth his wounded tongue failed him, and a gargled rumble went rolling through the church, echoing in the side-chapels.

Smallgods sat without moving, his arms along the back of

the pew, and waited for the priest to come to him, clicking down the aisle. When he was level with Smallgods, Damon turned and genuflected, and slid into the seat. He started to put out a hand to touch Smallgods' shoulder, and then retracted it, and put it out again, this time leaving it half-way between them. There was an expression on his face like that of a painted martyr.

Smallgods kept his eye fixed on the sanctuary lamp, and announced in a voice that was too loud for churches that he had come to collect his things, if that was all right.

Damon made a gurgle that sounded affirmative, and with spittle dripping from the corner of his mouth, made another gurgle that sounded like an apology.

'If you are saying what I think you are saying, don't. I'm not sorry. That's the trouble with your religion. You think you can do anything so long as you are sorry afterwards.'

Damon put his head in his hands, feeling the roughness and softness of his own hair and flesh, and forgot, for a perfectly happy moment, the existence of the bleeding Christ, and His elusive Father. The only thought in his head was that he was close enough to Smallgods Temple to touch him.

When he had roused himself, Smallgods was gone. The priest crossed himself, and wondered how to make a confession, if his tongue ever healed.

Smallgods stayed with Roland and Jean for a whole week, because John Donahugh's departure had been delayed. On Saturday, Jean said that she was going to extract some rent from him, and made him let her take a plaster cast of his entire leg. It meant that he had to stand on the draining board, wearing nothing but a shirt and a woollen scarf, supporting himself by resting his elbows on the wooden shelf behind. While she waited for the plaster to dry, Jean pushed squares of silk and calico and layers of onion-skin around in a steaming pot, which still bore the remnants of burnt potato about the rim.

'So tell me more about your friend John G.,' she said.

'John G.? What about him? I didn't know you knew about him.'

'You keep mentioning him.'

'Do I?'

A chickpea floated to the surface of the pot. Jean fished it out. 'I should have washed this pot first,' she said, and then she thought for a moment and dropped the chickpea back in, saying that she wondered what effect it might have on the colour of the cloth.

'I haven't seen him since Italy,' Smallgods said. 'Not since the summer. That seems like a long time ago. He must be at his agricultural college by now. We never said we'd write to each other. Is that better? School friendships aren't something you can carry over into real life. He is going to be a farmer. Live in the country and be a deep thinker and worry about the EEC and go up to Dublin for the Spring Show. By then I will be urban and unbearable. We will meet out hunting when we are both forty-five, and I am emaciated and affected, and looking out of place on a horse, after twenty-five years of associating myself with people like you. He will be fat with a red face, and say to other people in a low voice, "I used to go to school with that man with the long hair: you'd never think it, would you?"'

Jean said, 'You can be a terrible gobshite sometimes.'

'I know. But I don't hold it against myself. I'm very open-minded. I miss John G. a bit. You'd like him. He's your type. He treats me with the same sort of cynicism. I could ask him up to Limerick and you could seduce him. I'll be best man at your wedding. I think this plaster is set, and I have a cramp.'

Jean knocked on the leg, and listened. Then she took a huge pair of scissors and began to cut the plaster, working from his ankle towards his balls. Neither of them took any notice of the knocking on the front door.

Elsa knocked twice, and then found that the door was

open, and pushed it in. She could hear Smallgods giggling in the kitchen, and was about to call out to him, when she heard Jean's voice, so she went to the kitchen door to see what was happening. She saw her lover on the draining board naked from the waist down, while Jean fiddled the plaster from his leg.

She didn't wait to ask questions. In half a second she had gone out again and slammed the door behind her, and was rushing along the street as fast as her high-heels would allow. She was too angry to allow herself to cry in public.

'Was that Elsa?' Jean said. She hadn't looked around, only heard the click of high-heels.

'It was. I think she got the wrong idea.'

'Keep still. I should have put more Vaseline on you.'

'Do you think I should go after her? She might be throwing herself in the Shannon.'

'If you're lucky,' Jean said. 'She didn't seem like the suicidal type to me.'

'Don't you like her?'

Jean looked at him as if the question was mad, and then said, 'Everyone's allowed one mistake at your age.'

'She's moving in with me,' he said. 'In Mallow Street.'

'Are you in love with her?'

'Sometimes. She thinks I am.'

'I suppose you told her that.'

'She asks me at awkward times. I have to say yes. And there's the chance it might be true. I am and I amn't. What do you think?'

'Ask your friend John G.,' she said.

He sat on the draining board while he thought about that, and eventually he said, 'I see what you mean.'

Somehow, Smallgods explained himself to Elsa, and she left her husband and moved into the flat in Mallow Street with him. It might have been that she had already burned her boats in Tinnahinchy. She had told Jack that she was leaving him, but not why she was leaving him. She said that she was moving in with a friend. From his knowledge that his wife was not a sensual creature, he assumed that the friend was a woman, and so, while he threatened to break her jaw, he didn't see that it was necessary to follow his threat with action. The rumours in Tinnahinchy were that it was Elsa who had wounded the priest, and her departure was understood, to some extent, by the villagers. Jack thought that she would return when things had quietened down and there was a new curate.

There are two cities in Limerick. One is the old Irish city, on King's Island, and the other is the colonial city, laid out in a Georgian grid on either side of O'Connell Street. Mallow Street runs up to Pery Square and the People's Park, where the upmarket vagrants hang out, and banks of red salvia blaze in the summer, warding off anyone who is visually sensitive.

As John Donahugh considered himself to be a man of taste, his flat was almost bare of furnishings, except for a few bleak Victorian chairs and some Monet reproductions on the walls, and a tiny, original le Brocquy. There wasn't a looking-glass in the entire place, and Elsa and Smallgods spent a long time wondering how the owner had managed to shave himself, until Jean Spat told them that he had had electrolysis.

Elsa had some money saved, and they lived on that for the first few weeks. Smallgods discovered a source of fresh coriander and ricotta, and Elsa began to look for a job in the city. He persuaded her to buy a bottle of champagne to celebrate their first night. They argued in the shop, because she had seen what she thought must be champagne for three pounds a bottle, and he insisted on vintage Veuve Cliquot. In the end, he made her buy both kinds so that he could teach her the difference between what was worth drinking and what wasn't.

They sat on the rug in the sitting-room, surrounded by pomegranate peel. The ashtray was full of rock salt and she was wrapped around one of his legs.

'There's no more tomatoes,' Elsa said. She looked about fourteen years old.

'Are you glad you're here? Are you glad you're with me? Was it worth it?'

'Yes,' she said. 'Oh yes. What's that music called?'

'Mahler. Mahler's Fourth.'

'I thought Marlowe was a writer.'

'He was.'

'I'm glad,' she said. 'I wonder sometimes if I'm mad or dreaming or what. Sometimes I can nearly forget everything.'

'Forget what?'

'Jack. My Da. Sometimes I can nearly forget him altogether.'

'What times?' he said.

Because she had drunk all of the cheap wine, as well as some of the other, her tongue was softened, and her defences were lowered.

'Don't be asking,' she said. 'You're the only man who ever touched me and it didn't hurt.'

'You mean sex?'

'No. I just mean touching. If they touched me at all it was like they were hitting me. I used to want to scream sometimes, just from being in the same room as him. After I was seven. He started when I was seven. I had a maxi for my communion, and really long hair. I could sit on it, and everyone used to talk about it. Da used to brush it for me every night before I went to bed, even when we had visitors. He used to brush it for ages and ages, and he was always gentle. When Mammy brushed my hair she used to scratch my ears, but he was always gentle. He had itchy stubble when he kissed us all good-night, even the boys. He used to kiss them good-night too. Everyone said we were lucky to have such a nice Da. I used to hide in his lap when the boys were chasing me, and he'd smack them. He never smacked me. There was always a smell of stout off his breath, but I used to think it was a nice smell, before I was seven.

'But when I was seven, and the house was empty, except for him and me; Da and me; and he was brushing my hair and telling me that I was lovely, till I was nearly half asleep, and that was the best part. I would climb into his lap and he'd kiss me on the forehead, with his pricky chin against my eyelid, and the smell of stout. I had a long blue nightdress on. He picked me up, and put me on the floor, and I started to laugh because I thought he was going to tickle me. I remember laughing.

'He lay over me, and I didn't know what was happening, except that it hurt, and I told him to stop, and I was crying with the pain, but it was worse because I didn't know where the pain was coming from. But he wouldn't stop. He just kept saying soft things, and I cried until I screamed, and I screamed until I cried.

'He got the hatchet and showed it to me, and told me that it was a secret, and if I told anyone he'd kill me the way he killed the pullets. Or if I ever screamed again, he'd kill me. He used to tell me that he loved me while I was crying, but if my voice rose, he'd tell me that he'd kill me.

'My Da was dead after that. It was like he was a different man. He used to chant at me, "Stop it stop it I love it she cried."

'I got my brother Jamesie to cut all my hair off, and he got the strap for that, but still it didn't stop Da. When I was sixteen I married Jack instead.'

When she looked at Smallgods, there were tears in his eyes. She thought it must be love, and he let her think it. But while his eyes were wet, his mind was trying to work out the difference between love and pity.

'Times here I can forget it,' she said. 'I'm glad I came, but I don't like Marlowe.'

NOVEMBER

It was Friday evening in Roscarmony. When John G. came back from college, he found Mrs Temple sitting in the kitchen with Dervla, on either side of a pot of tea. He got the impression that he was interrupting something. The two women had an air of seriousness about them, which was not disguised by the cheerfulness with which they greeted him. Mrs Temple said that she had better be going.

At the door, Dervla said, 'I wouldn't worry too much about it. Call over any time. I'm usually here.'

John G. said, 'I'm sorry, Mrs Temple, I was going to ask you. Do you know what Smallgods' address is in Limerick?'

'Yes,' she said. 'I have it written down somewhere. I think it's in my bag. In the car.'

He went out to the van with her, and wrote the address down. Then the van wouldn't start, and he had to push it across the yard to get it going. She tried to thank him out of the open window, but he said, 'No, keep going, while the engine is running.'

Dervla was very quiet when he came back to the kitchen.

'What was all that about?' he said.

'All what about? Never you mind.' Later, she said, 'I'm glad I never married. That was one lucky escape.'

He handed her the evening paper, and while she looked over the death columns, he said, 'I was going to ask Dad for the loan of the Landrover and go up to Limerick tomorrow.'

'Jesus Mary and Holy Saint Joseph,' she said.

He thought she was objecting to his expedition, and was about to argue with her, when he saw that it was the paper she was exclaiming at.

'What is it?' he said. 'Who's dead?'

'God forgive me,' she said.

He stood over her, waiting for some explanation, but she seemed to be in a state of shock. Eventually she folded the paper, and said, 'It's nothing. It's someone I used to know at Trinity. I must write to him.'

'How can you write to him if he's dead?'

'Sweet Jesus, John G. Don't annoy me. It's his wife who's dead. I knew the two of them.'

'I'm sorry,' he said. He could see that there wouldn't be any point in asking her if she thought it would be all right about the Landrover, so he went to find his father.

John G. stood in the drizzle by the bus queue for Dooradoyle, outside Todd's in O'Connell Street. Unnerved by driving in the city traffic, he had already abandoned the Landrover. He was about to ask someone the way to Mallow Street, when Smallgods spotted him from the other side of the road, and began to scream out his name. At first he didn't hear, unaccustomed to the noise of a main street, and he saw Smallgods at the same time as he heard him, dodging between the cars in a long black coat.

'Hey, John G.! You deaf fart! Hey!'

Smallgods ignored the hooting cars, and ran over the road and the pavement, bowling his way through shopping bags and tinker children, and fell on John G. with what was nearly an embrace.

'Moore. You bollix. What are you doing in Limerick? I thought I'd seen the last of you.'

His voice was drawing stares from the women at the bus stop, and at first John G. was too stunned to respond. Eventually, he began to smile, and said, 'Hello. I thought I'd come up and see you. You don't mind?'

They went to Ma Hogan's pub first, and then back to the flat to see Elsa. Smallgods ran up the stairs, delirious, and dragging John G. by the elbow and sometimes by the coat.

Elsa threw her arms around Smallgods, and kissed him, and then she saw John G. and said hello in a cautious way. She was wary of Smallgods' friends.

'Elsa, this is John G. I told you about him.'

'Oh yes,' she said. 'He told me about you.'

She said it in such a tone that no one could speak afterwards, and Smallgods looked as though he wished the ground would open up and swallow him. Then she offered to make them tea, and disappeared into the kitchen.

When she returned, the other two were sitting down, and the bad atmosphere had been dispersed. They were laughing, Smallgods almost back in high spirits. She handed John G. his mug, and sat on the arm of Smallgods' chair, and put one hand down his jersey to fiddle with his shirt buttons.

'So you're the famous John G. Moore?' she said.

The other two sniggered at that. John G. said, 'I prefer to be called John. Just John.'

'Godfrey calls you John G.,' she said.

'Oh,' he said. 'Smallgods is allowed. I can't stop him.'

Elsa could see that she was being excluded from something, and she didn't like it when people called her lover Smallgods. She pulled a rubber band from her pocket, and began to put her hair up into a ponytail that made her look pre-pubescent, and then she fiddled with the straps on her high-heeled sandals. She thought that Smallgods was looking at her in a hard sort of way. She could feel his disapproval deepen when she said to John G., 'You've spilled your tea. I'll get you a serviette.'

'I was telling him about the party tonight in Shannon,' Smallgods said. 'He's brought a car, so we can go.'

'You can go without me,' she said. 'I'm not well.'

'What's wrong?'

'I'm just not well. I'm going to bed.'

As she went off towards the bedroom, Smallgods cast his eyes to heaven, and John G. studied the tea in his mug.

The party at Shannon Airport was being given by the Libyan Students' Friendship Association. It was mostly an exercise in anti-British propaganda, with a speech given by some sort of mullah about the common heritage of Libya and Ireland, and the threat to their sovereignty from British warships in the Mediterranean. Someone from the art school had been commissioned to paint a portrait of Colonel Gaddafi. The painting raised a lot of laughs, because it was photo-realistic, but cross-eyed. The Libyans, politely, couldn't say anything, because the painter was also cross-eyed, but they did what they could to mitigate it with Tippex and Biro.

The party, because it was Islamic, was to be dry, so everyone tanked up in Dirty Nellie's on the way out, and carried naggins of whisky in their pockets. More than that, when Smallgods and John G. called out to King's Island to pick up Jean and Roland in the Landrover, Jean fossicked in the freezer compartment of the fridge and produced some magic mushrooms, which she grilled on toast. John G. was doubtful about eating them, and would only have a few, but they were enough to distort his perspective for the evening.

So it wasn't a great surprise to him when, half-way through the party, while the Libyans were dancing to seventies disco music in their grey patent shoes, he found himself sitting on the floor in a dark corner kissing Jean Spat.

He was unaware of driving them home in the early hours, but he remembered Smallgods being offered the sofa in Jean's house, and it being assumed that he would go upstairs with Jean.

'I forgot to bring a toothbrush,' he said.

'You can use mine,' she said.

He could remember being embarrassed when she touched him in places he had never been touched before, and he could remember the nightmare thoughts that went through his head when he entered her for the first time. He felt as if his father and Dervla, and his mother and the parish priest were standing around the bed, but somehow he managed to go through with it. The first time was a disaster, but by the morning he felt as if he had been doing it for years.

He had to leave before ten. Dervla was expecting him for lunch. He promised to come back for more weekends, still not knowing whether Jean was now his girlfriend, or whether she did that sort of thing all the time. On the way out of Limerick he dropped Smallgods off at Mallow Street.

Smallgods met Elsa on the stairs. She was carrying a large suitcase. It was fake leather, the sort that you might store horse-rugs in if you didn't care what anyone thought. It seemed a coincidence that she should be leaving just as Smallgods arrived, but she had been watching out the window for him, to make her exit as dramatic as possible.

He said hello to her as she pushed past him. She was going down the stairs so fast that he thought she might trip on her heels and kill herself.

'Are you moving out, or what?' he called to her over the banisters, but there was no answer, only the sound of the suitcase thudding on the steps.

'ARE WE BEING EVICTED?' he shouted, just before the front door slammed behind her.

The tea was wet in the pot, and there was a cup still warm by the window, so he knew she had been watching for him, and he smiled at that. He poured a cup for himself and picked a copy of *War and Peace* from the bookshelf, which he began to read in the middle while he sat and waited for her to come back. This had happened once before.

When she did come back, she stormed straight through to the bedroom. She searched through his sock drawer, where she kept her tampons.

'Would you like to go for a drink?' he said.

She stood in the doorway, shaking.

'A drink. That's right. A drink.'

'It is after ten. The pubs are open.'

'I hate you,' she said. 'I hate you, you bastard.'

'I don't mind. Who you hate is your problem.' He knew that the best way to break her anger was to bring it to boiling point with arrogance. She picked up the milk jug and threw it at him. Luckily it was empty, and she was a bad shot. It landed on a cushion and didn't even break.

'I'm not coming back,' she said, and she left the flat again with a crash of the door.

'Good,' he said.

But the lower door on to the street didn't crash. When she came back again she was weeping. She had to sniffle several times before Smallgods looked up from his book.

'It is so hard,' he said, 'to work out who is who in Tolstoy.'

'God damn you,' she said. 'What are you going to do? You big shit. What are you going to do? Just sit and read your feckin' old book and do nothing? You're worse than bloody Jack Ponder. At least he doesn't pretend to be an intellectual. You're just the bloody same.'

Her cheeks were black with running mascara, and the hand that wiped them was red from dragging the suitcase downstairs.

'Oh bollix,' he said.

He threw the book down. He wanted to tell her how ugly she looked when she cried, but he didn't want her to know that he was angry now as well.

'Well?' he said.

She knew by now that that was as much of a compromise as she would get out of him, and she came closer to him. He stood up and put his arms around her. He wondered if the mascara would mark his jersey, and then nearly laughed at himself, because the jersey had spatters of paint on it anyway.

DECEMBER

The thing that John G. Moore disliked about Limerick most was the filth of it. Perpetual rain washed dirt on to the streets and off them again and into the Shannon. Every thing and human in the place was tinged with blackness, and when you came home, you carried the blackness with you, in your hair and on your shoes.

Unlike Wexford, which had a fair amount of sunshine, Limerick never seemed to see the sun, from one end of the winter to the other. Every time he visited, there was a pall of black cloud from the Atlantic hanging over the city. It was Smallgods, and Jean, who kept him coming back each weekend. If he could have chosen, he would never have returned to Limerick at all.

Sometimes, hardly ever, on a mid-winter afternoon, you might see the sun, sinking into the sea behind the coast of Clare. Except that you had to stretch your imagination to think that there might be a sea beyond Clare, or even that Clare might exist beyond the ugly houses out on the Ennis Road. The cold in Limerick made John G.'s bones ache, a thing he had never known in the cleaner climate at Roscarmony.

On Sunday morning, Jean would sit on a high stool, stirring the porridge, pushing back her hair and whistling through her teeth. Sometimes a hair would stray into the pot, and she would blow the steam away while her fingers darted in to retrieve it. John G. would sit on the stairs and watch her, clutching his toothbrush, while he waited for

Roland to finish in the bathroom. For someone who didn't seem to wash much, Roland spent a lot of the morning in the bathroom. Jean said that it was Zen and the art of bowel movement, which made John G. disinclined to use the lavatory after him, but there was no choice.

He thought, while he was watching her, that she didn't know he was there, but when the porridge was ready she began to speak to him, without turning round. He laughed, nervously. He was still a little bit afraid of her, even after three weekends of sleeping in her bed.

'What were you thinking?' he said.

'Nothing,' she said. 'I was thinking about Smallgods. Poor Smallgods. What do you think of Elsa?'

'All right.' John G. hadn't met Elsa a second time. He hadn't dared go back to the flat in Mallow Street, and when Smallgods came round on Saturday nights, he came alone.

'I thought,' he said, 'she seemed a bit young to be living with someone. What do her parents have to say about it?'

'Why? What age do you think she is?'

John G. shrugged his shoulders.

Jean said, 'Elsa is twenty-three. She is a married woman. But no children, I think.'

Before he could register his shock with any vocal expression, there was the sound of a lavatory flushing, and the rattle of the bathroom door. Roland came out, carrying a lifesized hardboard cut-out of a Friesian cow. He said no, he wouldn't have any breakfast. It was a fast day, and anyway he had to hitch to Tipperary.

John G. said, 'If you wait a couple of hours I could give you a lift. I'm going through Tipperary.'

'No,' Roland said. 'Thanks, no. I have to go now.' And he left the house, struggling with his cow.

'He'll never get a lift carrying that.'

'You'd be surprised,' Jean said.

Smallgods arrived in time for the porridge. John G. wanted

to be on his own with him, because he couldn't think of anything to say in front of Jean. Then Smallgods said that he was thinking of going home for a couple of days. They set off in the Landrover, looking out for Roland and his cow, but there was no sign of him. He must have picked up a lift straight away.

'Is Elsa really twenty-three?' John G. said it cautiously, trying to keep the accusation out of his voice.

'Yes. Why?'

'And married?'

'Oh for Christ's sake, yes.'

'You never told me.'

'Those things aren't important. If they were you would have asked.'

They were silent for the next few miles. John G. thought that Smallgods was sulking, but when Smallgods spoke again his voice was soft. It was hard to hear it over the noise of the Landrover.

'John G.?'

'Yes?'

'You know me. You know the way I am. If I were you I could talk, and it would all sound simple. I don't know which is the best way to be. If I could be as honest with you as you are with me, would everything be simpler, or more complicated?'

'Aren't you talking now?'

'No. That wasn't what I meant at all.'

They were slowing down through Clonmel. John G. said, 'I always thought you talked a lot more than me. A lot of the time you make me feel inarticulate.'

'That isn't what I mean.'

'What, then?'

'If I'm going to tell anyone, I should tell you. Elsa missed her period.'

'So? Isn't she pleased?'

'Pleased? Jesus Christ, she has enough to deal with already.'

108

'Sorry,' John G. said. 'I always thought periods were a hassle.'

'Seriously? You don't know?'

John G. was flustered and driving badly. They nearly went into the back of a lorry. Smallgods was laughing his head off.

'Let me tell you about the birds and the bees. Missed periods mean only one thing. Elsa might be pregnant.'

'A baby?'

'I don't know. It isn't certain. Maybe.' He was being serious again.

'So what will happen? You can't marry her if she's married already.'

'Nothing. What can happen? We aren't even sure she is pregnant yet. She always told me she was barren, so we didn't do anything about it. I don't love her, but she thinks that I love her. And there's a rumour in the school that I am going to fail the Christmas assessment. They don't like my attitude and my attendance is the lowest in the school's history. But they can't fail me, in fact.'

'Why not?'

'Because I'm going to quit first. Art is a dead-end. It's all hype and navel-gazing. Those aren't my sort of people.'

'So who are?'

'Stop asking questions. You're worse than a child.'

'Don't say that. I decided today. I'm not John G. any more. Even you can't call me John G. I'm John.'

He dropped Smallgods off and went back to Roscarmony. Dervla was seeing a visitor off in the yard. He was a sad-looking man with receding hair and a suit.

'This is Mark,' she said. 'Mark, this is John G.'

'I'm John,' he said. 'There's no G.' He said it abruptly, and when he had shaken the man's hand stalked into the house like an adolescent.

When her visitor had gone, Dervla had every intention of following her nephew, to make him apologise for his rudeness. But from the kitchen she could hear the thud of music being played loudly down in the sitting-room. She couldn't face walking into the wall of noise and seeing him splayed sulkily in a chair. She knew that a confrontation would only make her more angry. And she knew as well that she had to give some thought to her own situation. To get away from the beat of the music as much as anything, she put her Wellingtons on and went to see her mare and foal. It was almost time for them to be brought in for the night.

When she had written her letter of condolence to Mark O'Brien, she had tried to make it sound as normal as possible. She had spoken only of Liz, and her death, and the tragedy of dying young. She hadn't said that she would like to see him again. It would have been out of place so soon after the funeral.

The trouble with Liz's death was that it was a wish come true. Dervla remembered Mark and Liz's wedding, and having to smile and congratulate them, and at the same time hoping that Liz would die young so that Mark would return to her. She had kept an eye on the O'Briens in the death columns for seventeen years. It was the one evil thought she allowed herself, and the one sin she had never confessed.

Before she had come to Roscarmony to look after her sister's children, Dervla had been doing a line with Mark O'Brien in Dublin. He was studying history at UCD. Within months of her leaving Dublin, while he was still writing to her every week, his engagement to Liz was announced. He did well for himself; became a professor and wrote books about the decline of Greek civilisation. After the wedding they lost touch. When Dervla named her horses, she always had him in mind. The horses' names were like the jokes they used to share, and she thought that one of the days she would be able to make him laugh again.

He answered her letter by return of post. He said that

Liz had been suffering for a long time and her death was a merciful relief. He didn't say whether it was a relief to Liz or to him. He said that he might visit her some time, and talk about the old days. Dervla decided not to answer that letter for a while. She would wait until her thoughts were clearer, and until she could put something on paper that would not offend the sensibilities of a man who was recently widowed.

But he caught her out. He phoned on Saturday night and said that he would be passing through Kilnure on Sunday. What could she do but ask him to drop in for a cup of tea? His voice was exactly as she had remembered it.

From the moment he got out of his car, she knew that it was wrong. There was too much bitterness in her, and he had changed too much. He had lost his hair and his arrogance and his face had become fleshy. Once she had realised, standing by the back door, that this was not the man she had been in love with, she felt at ease with herself. She had no anger or passion to vent on the man who came towards her, picking his way across the yard like a townsman who is afraid of mud.

It was clear from his first sentence that he was looking for a new wife. Liz had been dead a month, but he said that it had been a long month, and the time had come to move on. He spoke like that, making his intentions plain, but never saying anything directly. He said that the children missed having a mother around. Dervla was almost insulted by that. She wanted to tell him that she had spent half her life already looking after other people's children; she wanted to tell him about her hysterectomy; tell him that if she couldn't have children of her own it was an offence to her that it was assumed she was available to bring up every orphan in the country. But she said nothing, only smiled and nodded in sympathy, as you would with a man who was bereaved, because at the back of her mind she knew that it would be stupid to burn her boats before she had a chance to think things over.

She knew that he wouldn't propose to her that day. Decorum meant that he would have to wait at least another six months. He was only preparing the ground. As he left he said that he would call again, and asked her to visit if she was ever in Dublin. She said that she only went to Dublin for the Horse Show in the summer. And then she added, 'Usually. I'll see.' They shook hands before he got into the car.

It was only after he left that she realised she hadn't told him the horses' names, or any of the things she had been saving to tell him over the years.

She brought the mare in from the field, with the colt capering and bucking up ahead, and the word that kept running through her mind was 'escape'. Here was her means of escape from Roscarmony, back to academic life in Dublin. She could probably take her up her degree again, and finish it. She would feel foolish in a room full of eighteen year olds, but that was not the worst ordeal she could think of. Once she had got used to Mark, and the way he had changed, she would probably fall in love with him again. He lived in Greystones; she could still keep a horse or two. By the time Clytemnestra and Orestes were in the box, she had almost decided to allow Mark O'Brien to marry her.

CHRISTMAS

Stasia Dwyer was dozing while she waited for her tin of biscuits. Mikey had gone to the pub, but left the door off the latch so that John could let himself in. He had to be called John now, or he wouldn't answer you. Even Dervla and Smallgods had learned to drop the G. Stasia had her rosary in her right hand and the remote control for the new television in her left. The beefeaters in plastic tubes had been joined by a flamenco dancer with pink-and-orange skirts. Because she had no plastic to protect her, she was getting rather dusty already. Otherwise Stasia's bedroom was exactly the same.

John coughed, and that didn't wake her. He hadn't the courage to shout at her the way Mikey would, so he stood at the end of the bed and waited for her to open her eyes, which she did as soon as the angelus began to toll on the television.

'God save ye. Are you there long?' she said. 'You should have woke me up.'

'You were asleep. Happy Christmas, Mrs Dwyer.'

He put the box of biscuits on the bed. She crossed herself for the angelus, and then zapped the television off.

'Great yokes these. Happy Christmas to you, boy.'

'You're keeping well.'

'Let me look at you. It's so long since I saw you. Would you not get that hair cut? You used to have lovely haircuts when you were little.'

'I like it like this.'

'I suppose it's the fashion.'

113

'No, it isn't. That's why I like it.' John scuffed his shoes on the rug and looked at his hands while he thought of something to say. He could have asked her about her health, but he couldn't face that monologue just at that moment.

She said, 'I hear you're great with young Temple these days.'

'I didn't know you knew him.' He said it defensively.

'Oh,' she said. 'I knew them years ago. When I was a girl I went to work in that house. It wasn't Temples in those days, it was Bridges. I worked for his grandmother for fourteen years. You want to watch those people. They're not a class of people to be trusted. They'll never change. All of the money and none of the manners. The ones that came over with Cromwell were bad enough, but the ones that stayed Catholic and hung on to the land were the craftiest.'

'That was a long time ago, Mrs Dwyer. They don't have any land now.'

'Things don't change,' she said. 'They're hard people. I wouldn't trust them as far as I could throw them.'

He was saved from arguing with her by the sound of the latch being raised on the outer door. His father came in, tapping softly on the bedroom door.

'God save all here,' he said. John winced.

'God save ye, boy, and a Happy Christmas. I was just telling this young fella about the Bridges at Ballynell.'

'A quare lot,' his father said.

John said, 'I'd better go. I haven't fed the horses.' He was going to glare at his father on the way out, for having betrayed his friendship with Smallgods Temple, but his father winked at him, and dissolved his indignation.

In the kitchen at Roscarmony Dervla was sitting at the table, staring at an unstuffed turkey, when John came in.

'Do you want a hand?'

'What? John, I didn't hear you coming in. No, I was just thinking.'

'I'll give you a hand if you like.'

'You couldn't,' she said. 'What do you know about cooking?'

'I cooked when your leg was broke,' he said.

She looked at him for a minute, and getting up from her chair she said, 'I suppose it's nearly time you learned. There's no guarantee that I'll be here for ever to cook for you.'

He felt himself turn cold. He thought she was talking about her eventual death. He had no idea that she could ever leave; that she wasn't as tied to Roscarmony as the barn in the haggard.

'You've a few years in you yet,' he said. 'I can make chocolate roulade. I learned in Italy. We don't have to have trifle tomorrow, do we?'

Already she was peeling sausages and chopping onions. She watched him set about making his chocolate roulade. Once or twice, she almost intervened with instructions, but she stopped herself. He seemed to know what he was doing, and to be taking pleasure from it.

'To think,' she said, 'that all these years I've been feeding you when you could have been feeding yourself as easily.'

'Do you remember Sarah,' he said, 'from last year?'

'We had a card from her yesterday.'

'I had a letter from her as well.'

'So what does she say?'

'She wants to know when I am going out to Australia for a visit.'

'Your dad is very shook.'

'I know. That's why I though I should go soon. While he can still manage things. If he got sick I wouldn't be able to go.'

'That's very heartless,' she said.

His face turned red. He thought he had expressed himself badly.

'No,' she said. 'I'm sorry. I shouldn't have said that to you. It isn't heartless at all. You're only young once. You'd be mad not to go to Australia while you have the chance. I suppose you'd go in the summer holidays.'

'I thought I might. Did I tell you that Smallgods was joining the British Army?'

'No. The British Army? What about his art school?'

'He changed his mind.'

Dervla snorted. 'That fella is a chancer. He takes after his father.'

'In more ways than one.' He regretted having said it instantly, realising that Dervla and Smallgods' mother were friends, and that Mrs Temple probably didn't even know of Elsa's existence.

'What?' Dervla said.

'Nothing. I just meant he was very stubborn; single-minded, like Oldgods Temple.'

'I meant his real father.'

'I know.'

'Do you want me to ask your dad about Australia for you?'

'No. Thanks. I'll do it myself.'

As Dervla stitched up the orifices of the turkey, she was thinking that it might be the last turkey she stuffed in that house. She wondered about saying something to John on the subject, but she still wasn't certain what would happen. There were days when she wasn't sure that she could be a married woman, having been herself for so many years. On the other hand, now that she had seen the possibility of leaving, Roscarmony and her life in it had become unbearable. She dreaded getting up in the mornings, and she began to hate small things, like the sight of the cattle passing the kitchen window. Her only confidante was Franny Temple, but Franny had problems of her own. Mark O'Brien had written to her twice since his visit, but his letters made her uneasy. He wasn't seducing her, but courting her, as if she was a farmer's daughter up for grabs.

John brought up the subject of Australia during the Christmas meal. It was just Dervla, his father and himself. Gerard had gone to London for Christmas. His father was indignant at that. Why his son should be going to London at a time when half the population of that city was desperate to get back to Ireland and couldn't.

John phrased his proposition badly.

'Dad, I was thinking of going to Australia.'

His father turned white and nearly choked on the chocolate roulade. In his mind people who went to Australia never came back. Once it was explained to him that John only had a two-month holiday in mind, he was so relieved and delighted that he began to joke about going himself.

'So you'll be staying with Sarah. What will that girlfriend of yours have to say about it? Jean, is it?'

John shrugged. He hadn't thought about that end of things.

'Jean won't mind,' he said. 'Sarah is only a friend.'

'That's not what I heard.'

John filled his mouth with food and said nothing. He was embarrassed that his father had heard from Mikey about him kissing Sarah on the marshes, but more embarrassed by the way in which his father was referring to it: there was something congratulatory about it, like being welcomed into a club.

It was that night that Dan Moore first saw blood in the lavatory. He had known for some time that there was something badly wrong with him, but he wouldn't admit it, or go to the doctor, because he thought that if he had cancer he would rather not know. He had seen people after radium treatment; people he had known while they were still strong. In his opinion the cure was worse than the cancer itself. And he had known people who had gone through the treatment and died anyway. He thought that if he was going to die he would rather do it on his own farm with his own hair on his head.

The blood in the lavatory confirmed what he had suspected. He thought he should go to a doctor now, if only to find out how long he had to live, so that he could make plans. In the bathroom, with the light on, he thought about these things rationally, and was surprised by his own courage. He had always assumed that he would be afraid of the prospect of death, when it came.

But back in the bedroom, in the dark, with the sound of his son breathing in the next bed, the fear stole up on him and gripped him. He started thinking about all sorts of irrational things that hadn't crossed his mind in years; about watching his children suck at the breasts of his wife; about watching John G. take his first piddle standing up. And then the fear got so strong in him that even those things wouldn't stay in his mind, and he lay on his side for the whole night, awake and shaking, with his hands pressed together between his thighs.

The next day he looked like a walking corpse. He decided that if nights like that were to be a regular occurrence he couldn't risk his son waking, and witnessing his ordeal. He told John that they should sleep in separate rooms. 'You'll be bringing girls home next,' he said. 'You won't want me looking over your shoulder.'

John's stomach turned. That remark was a bit close to the bone. More than once he had almost failed with Jean, because of the spectre of his father hanging over the bed.

'I don't mind,' he said.

Smallgods was in and out of Roscarmony over those Christmas holidays. Dervla lent him her horse for hunting on St Stephen's Day. He had worked himself up into a blind determination about the British Army and what a wonderful life it was going to be. Nothing to do but order people around for twenty years and then early retirement on a lieutenant colonel's pension. Dervla told him that he wouldn't last a week; that he should do something sensible, like horticulture.

He used to take John for walks in the dark, down to the river. Although Dervla said they were mad to be doing a thing like that in the middle of winter, they were the only times that Smallgods would talk with any degree of honesty. The rest of the time he was full of Army bravado and other nonsense, but when he was invisible in the dark he could almost be persuaded to speak in a normal tone of voice.

John said, 'What will happen to Elsa?'

'Elsa? What has Elsa got to do with it? She has gone back to her little husband in Tinnahinchy.'

'And he doesn't mind about the baby?'

'He doesn't know about it. There is no baby. It was a false alarm. She failed on that score.'

'Oh.'

'Listen. You aren't my wife. I don't have to tell you everything the minute it happens. I don't want to think about Elsa, or Limerick, or any of that. It was a waste of three months. Don't be so fucking neurotic. I don't want you making me feel guilty as well as everyone else.'

'What's there to feel guilty about?'

Smallgods made a noise of exasperation, and changed direction so that he was marching towards the bog.

'Don't go that way. You'll get stuck.'

Smallgods exploded. 'I'll get fucking stuck where I fucking want. I don't need you to nanny me. Look. If you have to know everything. I lied to you. As far as I know Elsa was pregnant, but she isn't now. As far as I know she took the boat. That's what we agreed the last time I saw her, and that's as much as I want to know.'

John was silent all the way back to the house. He couldn't think of anything to say that wouldn't have a high moral tone. But just as they reached the back door he spoke.

'Don't go to England. I'll miss you.'

'What am I supposed to do? I can't hang around in Ireland for the rest of my life just so you won't be lonely. It's all right for you. You have a farm and money and a decent father. If I want anything I'm going to have to earn it or steal it.'

JANUARY

Mrs Temple, several Deadlies, and John went to see Smallgods off at the Rosslare ferry. Smallgods had a leather bag with 'G.O.D. Temple' written on it.

'GOD,' John said. 'What are the O and the D for?'

'Godfrey Oliver David.' Smallgods smiled. 'But it isn't me. It's my father.'

'Son of GOD,' John said. 'How do you say goodbye to the Messiah?'

Smallgods kissed his mother, and the Deadlies, except Wrath, who wouldn't be kissed and kicked him hard on the shin when he attempted it. He put out his hand to shake John's hand, but it occurred to John that that would have been the stupidest gesture possible, and so he pulled on the hand and embraced Smallgods. It was very awkward. Neither of them had embraced a man before, but John felt better afterwards.

Wrath was screaming, 'Stop it, yez poofs! Everyone's watching.'

The man who clicked the tickets was laughing at them. He had been in the middle of telling a nervous woman that the sea was as smooth as a duckpond.

On the way back to the cars, Mrs Temple said to John, 'That was nice. I'm glad he has a friend like you.'

John had a double errand that day. On the way back from Rosslare he was to pick up Jean Spat from the train in Wexford town. He had been nervous about asking her down, about letting her observe him with his family; more worried about what she would think of his family than what his family would think of her. But Dervla was very good about it, and asked if she rode horses. John said that he didn't know, and phoned her to find out. She said that she did, so he told her to bring her hunting clothes. After he had done that, he felt ridiculous about the whole thing and wanted to cancel it. The point about Jean had been that she was part of another world. He wondered if he would still like her after he had seen her in a bowler hat.

When she got off the train she looked much as she always did, with her hair all over the place and her legs in black tights and paint stains on her jersey. When he saw her he almost felt compensated for the loss of Smallgods, and she had words of comfort as well.

'He won't last,' she said. 'He'll be back.'

When he introduced her to Dervla as Jean Spat, some of his worst fears were realised.

'Spat?' Dervla said. 'You aren't a Spat of Ballingsaggard? Is Paddy Spat your father?'

'Yes,' Jean said. 'Do you know him?'

'Of course I know him. I've known him for years. John has a horse that was bred by him. A Dunaris, out of Tiger Lily.'

Jean said, 'We still have the Tiger Lily.'

Dervla turned on John. 'You never told me you were going out with Paddy Spat's daughter.'

'I never connected,' he said.

'For God's sake, as if Ireland was crawling with people called Spat.'

After that it seemed to John that Jean was monopolised by Dervla. When he saw the two of them together, they seemed to some extent similar. John had never seen his aunt as someone who was still a young woman.

They had to creep down to the sitting-room to do it in the middle of the night, on the sofa by the lighted Christmas tree, because they would have been heard if they had been up to anything in either of their bedrooms. Sometimes, they had to stop, and be silent, because they heard soft footsteps on the landing above. It was John's father, prowling the house. He had begun to be in pain, and couldn't sleep at nights. On the fifth of January he went to Kilnure to see the doctor.

Dan Moore had never been in a doctor's waiting-room before. He had been ill once or twice, but the doctor had always come out to see him. He sat in a grey plastic chair and smiled at the coughing children. When it came to his turn, he had difficulty describing his symptoms. For a farmer, in daily contact with blood and excrement, he was surprisingly embarrassed when it came to describing the state of his own bowels. The doctor was a clammy young man with spectacles, not old Dr Flynn, who had been a friend of his and would have known how to put him at his ease. When he was asked to undress, he wished he had never come in at all. He could see that the indignities of illness were starting.

The doctor's hands were cool and damp, searching over his body, even the most intimate parts of it, as if he was the bran tub on a Fair day.

He was told nothing, except that he needed some tests. He would have to go to Dublin, to the Mater Hospital. The doctor made the arrangements over the telephone while he was still in the room, but nothing could be gleaned from what he said, because it was all in medical jargon and strings of initial letters.

He knew that when he got home he would have to say something to Dervla.

Everyone was right about Smallgods. He was back within a fortnight. But it wasn't because he had given up his ideas about joining the British Army. He arrived at Roscarmony without warning one Sunday afternoon, while John was following Dervla around her garden. She was looking for the first of the snowdrops. John was wearing Smallgods' long black coat.

She said, 'What are you doing with that old black thing on you?'

'I'm minding it for Smallgods,' he said.

'Minding it is one thing,' she said, 'but you don't have to wear it. Have you heard from him? Is he an officer yet?' She bent over what she thought might be an emerging crocus, making clicking noises at it to encourage it out of the ground.

'I don't know. He's hardly an officer yet.'

'Did you see your dad today? How does he look?'

'All right. I don't know. Maybe better. He went into town, but he didn't want me to come with him.'

'Please God he's a bit better, so.'

That was when Smallgods went flying past the wall on his bicycle. In another minute he had walked round the side of the house. His hair was shorter, but otherwise he looked the same.

'I knew you'd never stick it,' Dervla said.

They could both see that he was bursting with news, so John said that he had to go and put some silage down for the cattle, and took Smallgods away with him.

Smallgods said, 'You'll never guess where I'm going.'

'Australia.' John couldn't think of anywhere else that would be causing such excitement.

'I'll start at the beginning.'

John was about to start up the tractor, but he stopped and leaned over the wheel to listen to the story. Smallgods was sitting on the mudguard.

'I went to see my grandfather, to see if he could get me into his old regiment. It was the first time I'd ever met him. You should have seen him. Six o'clock alcoholic. He was perfectly normal during the day, but at about ten to six his hands would start to shake and at the first stroke of the clock he'd rush for the whisky bottle. Anyway. He said that I needed to have some of my corners rubbed off and learn the way the mind of the man in the street worked so that

I could give orders to squaddies without giving offence. So he said I had to go to the colonies for six months. I thought he meant Gibralter. I didn't know there were any colonies left, but he said Canada or Australia. So I said Australia, of course, and he asked me if I had any money, and I said no, so he gave me the money for the ticket. Do you know what else he said? He said it was a pity that my father never sent me to school; it would make things difficult with the Commissions Board, and I said that I had been to school, and he said that he hadn't meant a hedge school. A hedge school. Wouldn't you love to see the Christian Brothers' faces? I'm only back for a day, to pack; and then I've got to be at Heathrow on Tuesday. I'll still be in Australia when you come out in the summer. It's perfect,' he said. 'Perfect.'

FEBRUARY

Mark O'Brien came down to Roscarmony and proposed to Dervla on St Valentine's Day. She thought that it was taking things a little too far when he phoned and said that he would like to come and see her on the fourteenth, but she had no idea that the proposal would come so soon. She didn't want him coming to the house, because Dan was so frail, so she arranged to meet him in a hotel in Waterford for lunch.

She thought she was early, but he was there before her. He was wearing a new suit, and he had a bunch of roses by his chair to give her. She laughed when she saw the roses, but he took her laughter as gaiety, not derision.

'Do you like them?' he said.

She thought about telling him that she hated nothing more than scentless, long-stemmed, uniform, hybrid T roses wrapped in cellophane, but she remembered her manners and said, 'Lovely.'

She couldn't bear the flaccid way he gazed at her all through the meal, and the way he kept leaving his hand on the table, as if he expected her to reach across and hold it. After they had eaten, he ordered brandy for both of them without consulting her.

'Dervla, I was going to ask you something,' he said.

'What was that?' she said.

'I won't beat about the bush. I'd like you to marry me.'

'No,' she said.

She could see that he was more surprised than shattered.

'Is there something wrong? I know it's a bit soon after

Liz's death, but we don't have to tell anyone for a while. Would you like some time to think about it?'

'No,' she said.

'You can't say no just like that. Think about it at least.'

She felt her temper shorten. She knew that she was going to tell him things he wouldn't want to know.

'I've had plenty of time to think about it,' she said.

'How? I only asked you a minute ago.'

She thought that if he had been a child she would have slapped him.

'Allow me a little intelligence,' she said. 'I've had two months to think about it, and the answer is no.'

'You could at least tell me why.'

That was when she noticed the small black box in his hand. He must have taken it out of his pocket just before he proposed. She stared at the box until he was forced to put it back.

'You took a lot for granted, didn't you?' she said.

'Why?' he said. 'I want to know why.'

'You don't, really,' she said. 'But I'll tell you anyway. Look at me. I don't expect you noticed that I am still young. Not many people do. I'm thirty-seven years old. I've been in a state of suspended animation for the last eighteen years. I haven't changed. When I left Trinity to look after Dan and the children I thought it was only going to be for a term or two, and I thought you might wait for me. I might have, somehow, found a way of going back if you hadn't married Liz. Don't think I'm blaming you in this. There was pressure on me to stay at Roscarmony, and I stayed. It was my decision. Now look at yourself. I don't mean any offence, but you are an old man. Well, you look like an old man to me. You have had all the things I wanted for myself, and you won't want to do it again. I thought about marrying you. I don't love you any more, but I thought about marrying you for practical reasons. You won't be offended by that, I know; because I don't imagine for a moment that you love me, or ever did.

You are looking for a wife, not a lover. I laughed when I saw the roses because you looked so ridiculous as a Valentine. But I have one thing to be grateful to you for. When I thought that I might marry you, I thought about all the advantages, like living in Dublin and going back to university. When I decided that I couldn't bear to be married to you, it struck me that I could do all that anyway, without having to bring up your children or stand behind you at academic drinks parties. This is my last chance, and I'm not going to throw it away so that you can have a replacement for Liz.'

She was exhausted when she finished speaking, and she was worried that she had hurt him too much.

But he said, 'So that's a definite no?'

'Jesus Christ. I can see what drove Liz into her grave.'

He called for the bill, and said, 'Well, no hard feelings. I suppose, if you are moving to Dublin anyway, we can be friends.'

'It depends what you mean by that. If you are looking for a mistress, the answer is no.'

She could see that he was genuinely shocked by what she had said, and she relented. 'I'm sorry,' she said. 'I know that wasn't what you meant. No, no hard feelings. I suppose this hasn't been easy for either of us.'

He saw her to her car and they shook hands again as they had done in December. As she drove away, the thing that concerned her most was what to do with the flowers. She couldn't face the questions she would have to answer if she brought them home with her, so she stopped the car in Slieveroe and put them in a litter bin.

MARCH

John was worried about his father. Although no one had yet told him the full extent of Dan's illness, he knew that something was badly wrong. Dan had been up to the Mater twice and he was due to go up again. The evening before that last appointment, Dervla came into his room. He was reading a book about soil analysis for an essay he had to finish. Dervla sat down and said, 'You're late going to bed.'

'Fairly late. Why are you still up?'

He offered her some of his bar of chocolate, and she broke a bit off, and sat chewing it and staring at the radio, as if she was hearing one for the first time.

'Feck!' she said.

'What?'

'I bit my tongue.'

John laughed at her, and she began to laugh too. By the time they were calm again the atmosphere was less tense than the atmosphere she had brought in with her.

'Your father was bad last night.'

'I know. Do you think I should drive him up to Dublin tomorrow?'

'He isn't fit to drive himself. I've already told him that you have to go up to Dublin to get your visa for Australia.'

'I don't have to get it for months yet,' he said.

'I know,' she said. 'But don't tell your father that.'

She was staring at the radio again. She wanted to tell John about her plans for moving back to Dublin, for going back to university. She had already been in contact with Trinity, and every evening she looked over the lists of flats and bedsits in the evening paper. But it wasn't the right time to tell John about things like that, when there was so much uncertainty about his father. She would wait; there was plenty of time yet, between now and October.

When Dan came out of the Mater, the first thing he said was, 'Well, did you get your visa?'

'No,' John said. 'The embassy was shut. I'll have to come back another time.'

'That wasn't very organised of you.'

'I know.'

They were clear of Dublin before John could say, 'So, have they decided what's wrong with you yet?'

At first he thought his father wasn't going to answer, but then Dan said, 'Doctors are terrible fools.'

'I know.' John smiled. He was relieved to hear that, because he thought that it meant the illness, whatever it was, couldn't be so serious.

They stopped in Bagnelstown for a drink. Dan ordered pints for the two of them.

John said, 'I thought you weren't supposed to be drinking, and I'm supposed to be driving.'

Dan said, 'Doctors are terrible fools.'

John was thinking how much better his father looked: pinker than the corpse he had driven up to Dublin in the morning. He became certain that there had been good news from the doctors. They had a second round and John thought that they must be celebrating. His skull began to buzz because he hadn't drunk pints of beer for a long time. By the third round his head was reeling, but he didn't know whether it was from the drink or from happiness. He was thinking of his father cured and strong again and of spending the summer in Australia with Smallgods.

Then his father told him a joke that he had heard from one of the other patients in the waiting-room, and by the fourth pint the two of them were laughing so much that they had to hold on to the counter.

When they were on their way again, somewhere before Thomastown, they were being more serious. They were talking about Australia.

His father said, 'Before you go up again for your visa, there's something I should warn you.'

'What?' John said. He was thinking that his father was going to warn him about sunbathing too much and getting skin cancer or something like that.

'I was told today that I have three weeks to live. Maybe a bit more.'

Because he began to shake, John thought that the thing to do was to put his foot on the accelerator, and he also thought that if he drove fast enough the last sentence would be left behind them on the road. When he had to slow down for Thomastown he was shaking so much that he could hardly keep the car straight. He stopped, and his father took over the driving. There wasn't anything that either of them could say the rest of the way to Roscarmony.

EASTER

Dan Moore died when spring was pushing through the ground and the bottoms of the hedges were turning green. Dervla was with him when he died, and John was in the next room in bed. It was between two and three o'clock. John had been having a dream in which someone asked him how his father was. Before he could answer, a voice from behind him said, 'Dan is dead.' He woke up when he heard those words, and lay in the dark for a few moments, relieved that it had only been a dream. Then a black fear crossed his mind, and he knew that his father was dead in reality.

He got out of bed and went to his father's bedroom. Dervla was holding the hand of the corpse. She had just closed his eyelids.

John stood in the door, and spoke. 'He's dead.'

It was so quiet that he could hear Dervla make a swallowing noise in her throat. 'God rest him,' she said. 'Go back to bed. There's nothing can be done until the morning.'

He obeyed her, automatically, but half-way down the landing his knees gave way and the world went black. From the bedroom, Dervla heard the thud of his body falling on the carpet.

John knew nothing of the funeral. He had vague memories of Gerard and Mary Howlin and one or two other relations coming into his bedroom from time to time. In his more lucid moments, he asked Dervla to keep them all away, but some of them insisted all the same. The doctors told him that what was happening to him was normal, and prescribed more drugs. He had a fixation that he had to speak to Smallgods, but when he phoned Sarah's number in Australia she said that she hadn't seen him yet.

APRIL

Sarah came haring through the bush, kicking up dust in streams from the wheels of her Tojo. She bounced along over the rocks, leaning forward over the steering-wheel, her eyes clinging to the ground ahead. Beside her, an Aboriginal sat, calmly jolting from his seat to the ceiling, lighting matches and flicking them out of the open window into the clumps of dry grass that were scattered over the terrain. Whenever he hit one, the grass would burn quietly for a moment or two, and then shoot up into an obelisk of orange. Neither Sarah nor the Aboriginal turned to watch the flames, but as they drove on they left an avenue of torches behind them. Otherwise the landscape was deserted. In the distance, red and yellow hills rose in front of a pale-blue sky. A flock of parakeets emerged from the scrub and flew in circles.

A hundred miles south, Smallgods Temple sat across his bag while, behind him, the early-morning sun crawled over the nape of his neck, and the early flies dived at his face. The road by which he sat went a hundred miles south and a hundred miles north between that place and the next. He was watching the road to the south for signs of life.

A long way off, a column of dust rose in the air, and fifteen minutes later a filthy white Ute could be made out coming towards him. It was the first car he had seen since the night before. Behind the Ute, billows of red dust were suspended in the air for two miles. Smallgods waited until it was a quarter of a mile away, and then straightened his legs out like someone rising from the dead. He uncurled his back until he was standing straight, still with a leg on either side of his bag and his thumb pushed out into the sunshine. His face was devoid of expression. He knew better than to look as if he was pleading, hitch-hiking in Australia.

The driver, whose face was burnt purple, slowed his Ute and came abreast of Smallgods. He leaned across the front seat and shouted out of the open window. A normal tone of voice would have done, but in that climate people shouted.

He asked Smallgods where he was going, and when Smallgods told him, he laughed, and asked how long Smallgods had been there.

'Since last night.'

'It could be worse. I seen 'em here three or four days sometimes.'

And then he laughed again and drove away, leaving Smallgods in a cloud of red dust.

The day dragged on, and Smallgods began to walk, changing his bag from one shoulder to another every half mile or so, wondering if he could last the hundred miles with no water. In the afternoon, every couple of hours, a car loaded with tourists and luggage would pass. Those people never stopped, but some waved to him. Others pointed their cameras, thinking that he must be a swagman. The road was dotted with the corpses of dead kangaroos and bullocks, and the more recent ones had to be given a wide berth, because of the flies.

Towards dusk, a roadtrain stopped. His mouth was so dry that he couldn't speak to explain where he was going, but the driver opened an eskie and gave him a carton of strawberry milkshake. There was the occasional thud of a beast being killed on the front of the vehicle, but they were sitting too high up to see anything of it, except the odd splash of blood on the windscreen. It was late evening when he was dropped at the turning for Boogiwarra. There was only another eight miles to walk before the house.

Half-way there he put his bag down and went behind

a bush for a pee. It wasn't until he had finished that he realised how ridiculous his modesty had been, in the dark with no human for miles. In another state of mind he would have laughed at himself. Because there was no one to hear, he said aloud, 'Fuck it, John G. Moore. I need you.'

MAY

Just before his birthday, John began to behave normally. He had decided that if he was mad the best thing to do was disguise it. He wasn't going to be taken away as his mother had been. Getting out of bed in the mornings was the hardest, but the backlog of work on the farm kept him from thinking during the daytime and exhaustion claimed him in the evenings. He was told the details of his father's will, in which the farm was left to him in its entirety. Gerard and Dervla got some money. He felt bad about Gerard. He wanted to contact him and see if he could make amends. But Dervla said that Gerard had gone to London and not left an address.

Dervla made him a cake for his birthday, and he blew the nineteen candles out, and she cut two great slabs and put them on plates. Then they sat, facing each other, watching the oozing chocolate on their plates. It was all he could do not to revert to his previous state. He couldn't open his mouth to take the cake in, because he knew that once his mouth was open a sob would break out of it. He wasn't ever going to show anyone the symptoms of madness again. With a great effort of will, he pulled his mind out of his body, and watched himself and Dervla sitting at the table. He thought: This is schizophrenia. But it doesn't matter, so long as no one knows but me.

For the rest of the evening he watched himself speak and move. Sometimes he tried to order the way he spoke or moved, but found that he had no control over himself. He could watch his hand resting on his knee, and if he tried to move it it wouldn't. Later, it would move of its own volition, when he had stopped paying attention to it.

Jean Spat phoned. She said that she had been phoning Dervla while he was ill. He heard himself talking to her in what he thought was a normal voice. But when she heard the tone of his voice, she said, 'I'm coming down to see you. Don't do *anything* until I get there. Just wait. I'll be there tomorrow.'

He heard himself laughing, and saying that he didn't know what she meant, and he said goodbye to her as quickly as he could. When he had put the phone down he knew that there wasn't much time. If Jean came she would be able to see that he was mad. He couldn't hide anything from Jean. Once it was known he was mad he would be taken away.

He watched himself cross the yard in the dark and go up into the hayloft above the stables. He had been careful about leaving the house so that Dervla wouldn't notice. He lay in the straw on the floor of the loft and listened to the horses snorting and eating.

Then the light went on, and Dervla came into the stables. At first he thought that she had come to look for him, but she went into the box where Odysseus was and began to talk to the horse. He couldn't make out what she was saying, only that she sounded miserable. He thought: She is mad as well. She talks to horses. It is in the family.

He was aware that there was hot water flowing from his eyes across his cheeks, and he realised that he must be crying but he couldn't think why. He put it down to another symptom of madness.

He watched Dervla go back across the yard in full moon-light. The clouds had gone and there was a fat moon shining on the landscape. While he was still watching the moon he was aware that his body had got up from the straw and was climbing down the loft ladder. He thought he would follow it out of curiosity.

He watched himself walk down to the marshes, his hair turned the colour of pearls in the moonlight. He seemed to be walking the marshes in the direction of Ballynell. After about half a mile he came to a stream that couldn't be crossed without going up on the headland and coming back again, but instead of going that way he turned and walked towards the river. That was when he realised what was happening. The river hadn't had her quota of three corpses yet that year. He wondered whether he really meant to drown himself, or whether he meant to swim to Ballynell. But he felt so disconnected from the action that he thought it was none of his business.

He could see himself undressing. His arms were brown for three-quarters their length from driving the tractor, and apart from his face the rest of his skin was a translucent non-colour in the moonlight. The hair below his navel was pearl, like the hair on his head. His feet seemed to be a long way down.

The hedges stank of May. You could smell them even across the putrid marshes, their sweetness cutting through the acid bog. He stood on a hummock with his toes grasping in the tough grass, and then he began to walk into the river.

Although it must have been deep near that bank, the water seemed to swallow him by inches to his thighs. The cold hit him first on his balls and then there was half a splash. The other half of the splash must have been heard above the surface of the water, but his head was below it. His feet sank into mud, and then he began to glide and the cold seeped into the rest of his body. He watched himself feeling all that.

His arms began to pull strokes towards the middle of the river, and then upriver, in the direction of Ballynell. It was hard to say how long it was before he tired of swimming against the current, but the last thing he remembered thinking was that the water was cleaner than you might expect.

There was a sort of click that was almost audible, and John

was back within himself, cold, and clinging to the slime of a salmon trap. He realised that he didn't know how long he had swum or floated down the river. He could have been carried for miles. The sky had clouded over again and he could see nothing but the bulk of the riverbank twenty feet away and the white of his own shoulders above the water.

He couldn't understand why he hadn't drowned. By now he should have been floating out past Passage East and Hook and Crook. He began to be afraid, but afraid in a rational way that seemed dangerously like sanity. His legs were clasped tight around the sticks of the salmon trap and the cold was becoming too severe to be bearable. He decided to swim for the bank. From the flow of the river he knew that he was on the Wexford side, not the Waterford, and that was lucky. It was lucky, too, that the tide was coming in, and he was on the bank in ten or fifteen strokes. Then he lay in the rushes, frozen.

He tried to judge where he was, but it was too dark. He thought he must be as far as Dunbrody at least. The idea of walking home naked along the roads was so alarming to him that he thought about getting back in the river again. He began to walk towards the bulk of the headland. The rushes were sharp on his bare soles, and when he wasn't holding his hands out to balance himself he cupped them over his genitals in an attempt at warming them.

In the first field he came to, he could hear the sound of horses breathing. He hissed through his teeth and the horses came closer. He spoke to them. If he could identify the horses he would know whose land he was on and how far away home was. One of the horses came up to him and put its chin on his shoulder and began to lick his ear. You could tell it was a young horse by the way it was slobbering.

Then a bit of the moon came out. Enough to convince him that the horse was Orestes. He would know for sure if the other horse was Oedipus. They had been turned out together while the colt was being weaned. He called, and the other horses came up to him. He was only three fields from home.

Orestes licked his back while he wrapped himself around Oedipus's shoulder for a bit of heat, then he vaulted on to the horse's back and rode him to the gate, the colt alongside nibbling at his feet and muzzling his calf.

Despite what she had said on the telephone, Jean Spat borrowed a car and drove down to Roscarmony that night. She had shared a flat once with a girl who had killed herself, and there was something in the tone of John's voice that alarmed her. She had no idea what she could do once she got to Roscarmony, or how she would explain herself.

The roads were clear and she drove fast. She was there in less than two hours. The house was in darkness except for a light in the kitchen. The back door was open. She tapped her fingers on it and let herself in. Dervla was at the table kneading dough for brown bread, and listening to a radio play.

'I thought I heard a car,' she said.

'I told John I was coming down. Where is he?'

Dervla thought for a minute, and realised that she hadn't seen him for several hours. She concluded that he must have gone to bed.

'He's gone to bed,' she said. 'He should have stayed up if he knew you were coming.'

'He didn't think I was coming until tomorrow.'

'That must be it, so.'

Jean was about to ask if she could go up and see him, but already Dervla was wiping the flour from her hands and saying, 'You must be hungry after your long drive. Sit down and I'll get you something.'

Jean hesitated, and then sat down. She thought that at least she should go through the formalities of condolence before she went rushing up to John's bedroom.

'I was sorry to hear about John's father,' she said. 'It must have been a great blow.'

Instead of answering, Dervla turned away from her. Jean got up and came around the table to embrace the shoulders of the weeping woman, and guided her into a chair.

When Dervla had been crying for several minutes, she wiped her face with the tea-towel and said, 'I'm sorry.'

'There's nothing to be sorry for,' Jean said.

'There is. I'm being selfish. I shouldn't be thinking about myself at a time like this. This isn't grief. It's pure self-pity.'

Jean said, 'If you can't pity yourself there isn't much chance of being able to pity anyone else.'

It was that remark that gave Dervla confidence in her, and she told Jean everything: about Mark O'Brien; about going back to university; about how Dan's death had foiled all her plans and condemned her to go on living in Roscarmony. Jean said very little until she was finished, and then tried to make her see things in a more practical light.

'You might have to put it off for a year,' she said, 'but I don't see why you can't go through with it. You'll have long holidays and weekends to be here if John needs help. You might be surprised how little help he needs. He's less of a child than you think. He's less of a child than he knows himself. If things go right you might even manage to go up this year. We'll work it out somehow.'

'We?' Dervla said.

Jean said, 'Just wait and see what happens.'

When he reached the house, he saw that the light was still on in the kitchen and there was a strange car in the yard. The only other way in was through the bathroom window over the porch. There was a danger that if he made a noise it would be heard in the kitchen and he would be caught naked on the porch roof, by Dervla and God knew who else. If he was seen in that state, the asylum was a certainty.

As silently as he could, he pulled himself up on to the roof and crept across it on his hands and knees. The bathroom window was stuck, and he began to panic, but eventually it gave way, and shot up with what seemed to him a deafening noise. He tumbled into the bathroom and turned the light on. He was covered in mud, and his feet and legs were badly scratched. As quickly as he could, he wiped the worst of the mud off with a face-cloth and made a dash for his bedroom, flushing the lavatory first to cover himself.

Below in the kitchen, the two women looked towards the ceiling.

Jean said, 'He's awake. I'll just go up and see him.'

When she got to his room he was already in bed, with the covers pulled up to his chin. From what she could make out in the light from the landing he was in a deep sleep. There was something calm in his breathing that reassured her, and she decided not to wake him.

JUNE

Because the child had been conceived in September, when Elsa Ponder went back to live with Jack he had no suspicion that it wasn't his. He had always assumed that she was the one who was infertile. She wouldn't let him come near her any more, but that was understandable to him since she was pregnant. Because of the child he was prepared to forgive her and pretend that she had never been away. He still thought that she had been staying with a girlfriend in Limerick. There was a new curate in the village, and Jack even suggested that she should apply for her old job.

She managed to stay with him over Christmas and the New Year, but by the end of January she was rigid with despair. She tried writing to Smallgods at his home address but he didn't answer. She called at Jean and Roland's house to get news of him and was told that he had gone to Australia.

Without telling Jack, she applied for a chambermaid's job in a small hotel on the north side of Dublin. When she went up for the interview, her pregnancy wasn't showing too much. She got the job and started straight away. Board and meals were provided. For the next four months she never left the building. On her days off she watched television in her room.

The pregnancy began to show, but by that time the woman who owned the hotel had become a friend of hers, and her job was secure. Towards the end she was given only light duties. It was the owner of the hotel who organised a hospital bed for her, and drove her there when the time came.

The baby was a girl. She was named Patricia, after the owner of the hotel.

JULY

At Dervla's invitation, Jean spent her summer holidays at Roscarmony. She helped on the farm and carried on with her own projects as well. She had brought a spinning-wheel with her, and she gathered lumps of fleece from the hedges and fences and spun and dyed them. At first, she stuck to her vegetarian principles, but one Sunday the smell of roast beef was too much for her and she relented. John was surprised that Dervla made no comment when Jean began to sleep with him in his bed. He wanted to ask one of them if it had been arranged between them, but he was half afraid of uncovering some sort of conspiracy.

Since his night in the river he was back in control of himself. There were times when he was consumed with fear. He had no explanation for this fear. It was if a black hole opened in front of him, and he couldn't see any hope or future or love in the world. Often this fear was preceded by him thinking about eternity, in the scientific sense; about what was beyond the known universe and what had preceded time. In its texture, this fear was not very different from the nightmares he had had as a child. But now it came to him only in his waking hours. At night, the presence of Jean, wrapped around him in the summer heat, kept the fear away.

He had bouts of inexplicable happiness too, and they became more frequent as the summer progressed. He worried about this happiness; that if Smallgods returned to find him happy, he wouldn't know how much he had suffered. He thought about Smallgods' return every day. There were things that he wasn't able to say to Jean or Dervla. Towards the end of July, Smallgods phoned to ask him to meet him in Italy in August. He had to refuse, because he couldn't leave the farm, but the phone-call itself left him elated for days. It was his first contact with Smallgods since January.

AUGUST

Smallgods had worked on the station at Boogiwarra until the Fortesque Races. He was living in Perth now, or rather a suburb of it called Nedlands, near the university. As the heat increased, he spent most of his days out on the beach at Scarborough or Swanbourne. He bought running shoes, and in the mornings he could be seen in shorts with all the other joggers, running by the Swan River, between the palm trees, as far as the Mitchell freeway and back. The girl he was living with worked for a car-hire firm. At weekends they drove into the bush to look at the spring flowers. But he was getting tired of her. She was a creature of routine. He lied to her, telling her that he was due back in England, and left three weeks before he needed to. She wept and told him that she loved him, but he told her that he was signed into the Army and if he didn't go he would be arrested for desertion. Then he went to the airline office and exchanged his ticket to London for one to Milan. He had, in fact, decided not to join the Army after all.

On his way to the airport, he stopped in the city centre and bought some haematite cuff-links for John, and a boomerang for Wrath. On his flight, drink was included in his ticket. When he reached Malpensa Airport twenty-one hours later he was a little bit drunk, but not jet-lagged, because the flight was west to east.

He had tried to telephone his uncle to warn him of his arrival, but the number was out of order. He was not alarmed, since that was not unusual in Italy. There had been no real need to telephone ahead in any case, since the house was always given over to his family for the month of August.

He stood before the house in Busto Arsizio. The front door was open, but the house had a look of desertion about it. He looked over the hedge to Fabio's pool, but that too was bereft of people. He thought that everyone must have gone to Como for the day. He had the house to himself for the afternoon. He pushed through the door and dropped his bag in the hall. A woman appeared on the stairs. She was stout and middle aged with large gold ear-rings. He assumed that she must be a new maid his uncle had employed.

'*Ciao*,' he said, and smiled at her, and went to the kitchen to make himself some coffee. As he searched for the espresso pot he realised that he should have asked the woman where his family was, and what time they would be back. Looking about the kitchen, he began to realise that something was wrong. There were scarlet mugs hanging on a wooden tree. He thought that someone must have taken leave of their sense of taste. It made him cross to think that anyone he was related to could have bought mugs like that. Then he heard a noise behind him.

The woman was standing in the doorway, behind a small man with a large nose. They both seemed a little agitated. The man asked him who he was and what he was doing. He answered, rather imperiously, that he lived there, and who were they? The man looked back at the woman, and she made a sign by the side of her head to indicate that Smallgods might be mad. Then she prodded the man in the back to suggest that he should do something about it.

It slowly dawned on Smallgods that the house had been sold, and that these people were the new owners. He gathered what remained of his dignity and excused himself; picked his baggage up from the hall and went next door to Fabio's house.

Fabio Arnolfini was at home. 'Of course,' he said. 'I

had a terrible fight with your uncle about the people to whom he sold it. I will never forgive him. Did you see them? Gucci and sunlamps. What the English call upwardly mobile. First-generation cuff-links. If your uncle had been so desperate for money, I would have bought the house from him rather than have people like that next door.'

'Why did no one tell me? I had a letter from my mother last month and she never mentioned it.'

'Your mother is what I think is called vague. I am going to make an enormous bank on that side of the garden. Four metres high so that I can see nothing of them. And plant it with some impenetrable thorn bushes from South America. The bulldozer comes on Wednesday to start the work.'

'I'm sorry,' Smallgods said.

'Sorry? Why should you be sorry? It is your uncle I won't forgive. Now, how long do you want to stay with me? You can stay as long as you like.'

'Thanks. I don't know. I wasn't planning this.'

'Well,' Fabio said. 'Just stay until you have to be somewhere else. I heard you were going to join the Army.'

'That's all off.'

'I'm so glad. You wouldn't have liked it. All that shooting. And the British are being beastly to the poor Argentinians just now. It isn't fair really. Argentinians, like Italians, are much too civilised to be good at war. The English will win. They are the playground bullies of the world.'

Smallgods stayed with Fabio for five days. The trouble began on the fourth day, and it was the reason Smallgods left on the fifth.

On the morning of the fourth day, he was woken by Guido, who was standing on the gravel beneath his window and shouting for him. Guido was the more interesting of Fabio's gardeners. He was an ex-junkie from Sicily. He wore his hair long with a revolutionary red headband and he had a handlebar moustache. In the summer he wore red underpants and nothing else. He lived in a small house in the village with his wife and twelve children. While he was at home, the house shook with songs about Sicilian independence. Sometimes he put the speakers outside the window to annoy the Piedmontese. The only words of English he knew were 'fuck', 'friend', and 'smoke'.

Smallgods struggled to the window just as Guido had picked up a handful of gravel and was about to throw it into his bedroom.

'Hey,' Guido shouted. 'Smoke?'

He fished in his red underpants and produced a joint, and then did a mime of inhaling it and staggering about on the gravel. His skin was almost black with the tan and the texture of shoe leather.

'*Dove* Fabio?' Smallgods said.

Guido shrugged. Plainly Fabio was away for the morning.

Guido took Smallgods to the toolshed, which was hung with communist posters on the inside. By half-past nine, they had smoked two large joints and drunk a litre and a half of terrible wine. Afterwards, Smallgods went and vomited in a fountain, where carp rose to the unexpected feast. Guido seemed unaffected by the morning's excesses.

Without warning, Guido scampered off into the bushes. Fabio was strolling up the avenue, between the ambling macaws and Amherst pheasants. When he reached Smallgods, he said, 'Was that Guido I saw a moment ago?'

Smallgods said, 'If you paid him better, he might be able to afford better wine.'

Fabio was wrinkling his nose at the mess in the fountain. 'If I paid him any better, he would be permanently drunk and I would have to sack him. I couldn't have all those starving children on my conscience. I think it is time for a swim, if you promise not to vomit in the pool.'

'I can't guarantee it.'

As they were walking towars the pool, Fabio said, 'Whatever happened to your friend? What was his name? The tall blond stupid one. You must be careful if you choose your friends for their looks and not their minds.'

Smallgods spoke crossly. 'John isn't stupid. He has one of the best minds I know. Besides, one doesn't choose friends. They happen.'

'Like lovers?' Fabio was being more malicious than usual.

'No, not like lovers. Lovers are transitory. Friends last you your whole life.'

'You are so young sometimes,' Fabio said, and laughed. They walked on in silence, stopping sometimes to admire a new tree, or watch a macaw destroy an old one.

Smallgods felt too ill to swim, so he sat in the shade while Fabio lay in the shallow end of the pool where it was only three inches deep. The wavemaker hummed and a spider monkey groomed Fabio's chest-hair.

Smallgods said, 'Do you know why my uncle sold the house and moved?'

'Your uncle? Oh yes, I see what you mean. Your uncle. Really, I think you are getting too old for these, these – what is the word in English for when you use a harmless expression to disguise a disgraceful one? Although I don't know what you would call him if you didn't call him your uncle. You could just refer to him as Julian, perhaps? I understand that a lot of children do that these days.'

'What are you talking about?'

Fabio raised himself on his elbows with an expression of mock surprise. 'Do you mean they have never told you?' he said.

'Told me what?' Smallgods asked it in spite of not being sure that he wanted to know. What made him most uncomfortable was the pleasure Fabio was taking from the revelation he was about to make.

'I'm sure you must have suspected it. All firstborn children count the time between their parents' marriage and their birth. In your case the marriage happened after the birth.

The fact is that Julian is your real father. Oldgods stepped into the breach to save your mother from disgrace. Poor man. I hear he wanted to be a priest really. He and Julian are so different that you wouldn't think they were brothers.'

He continued, but Smallgods wasn't listening. When Fabio had stopped speaking, all Smallgods said was, 'You needn't have told me that.'

Having done his damage, Fabio was all kindness and charm for the rest of the day. He offered Smallgods some cocaine in the evening, and Smallgods was grateful for anything that altered the state of his mind. Before they went to bed, Fabio, as usual, almost as a matter of form, propositioned him. As usual, Smallgods said no, and said good-night.

He was gone when Fabio woke the next morning. He hadn't left a thank-you note, and since he hadn't any money it was assumed that he was hitch-hiking back to Ireland.

THE THIRD YEAR

SEPTEMBER

Smallgods returned to me on the second or third. Dervla was making plans to go back to Trinity in October, and Jean's final year at Limerick Art School was due to start in the second week of September. When Smallgods came back, Jean was already in Limerick, finding somewhere to live. It was arranged that Philomena Dwyer, a niece of Stasia's, would come in for four hours a day to clean the house and make the dinner. I said that I could cook for myself, but Dervla said that I wouldn't have time with a farm to run. But she took my hint about not wanting to live on a diet that was exclusively spuds, cabbage and bacon, which was all that Philomena would have provided, and Dervla spent most of September filling the freezer with enough food to take me up to Christmas.

I said that Smallgods returned to me, because when he reached Rosslare he telephoned here and asked if he could stay at Roscarmony. He said that he couldn't go back to Ballynell. Not only did I say yes, but I got into the car straight away and went down to Rosslare to collect him.

I couldn't describe to you how excited I was as I drove down. His return was going to make up for everything. I had visions of throwing myself around him in an embrace that would dissolve all the depression and all the madness; of him taking me for walks in the middle of the night so that I could tell him things that no one else would have listened to.

I don't know what went wrong. He was standing by his bag

in the ferry car-park, and at the sight of him all my courage left me. I smiled, of course; and he grinned back. But I didn't even have a chance to get out of the car. He came straight round to the passenger door. It was like being a taxi-driver, and not how I had imagined picking up Smallgods Temple would be.

Before, his sophistication had always made me feel like a child, but now, I felt uncomfortably adult. He was a drifting hitch-hiker, and I was a farmer in a BMW. And at the same time, instead of giving me pleasure, the sight of him filled my head with reproaches. I tried to suppress them for as long as I could, but by Wexford town they were battering their way on to my tongue. I tried to sound as nonchalant as possible.

'You never wrote,' I said.

I could sense him smiling. I looked across at him to check. It was that smile that could dissolve any bitterness you felt for him. I had forgiven him even before he answered.

'I did,' he said. 'After I heard that your father had died, I tried writing several times, but I never got to finish the letters. What could I have said?'

'I know what you mean. I tore up a lot of the letters I wrote to you. Did you get the letters I sent to you at Sarah's?'

'All forty-three of them.'

'Sixteen were written on the same day.'

'I noticed.'

'Well you're here now,' I said.

I almost took the turning for Ballynell by mistake, before I remembered that he was coming to stay with me.

I said, 'So what's up at Ballynell? I noticed your family didn't go to Italy this year.'

'Don't ask,' he said. And then, 'Well, I suppose if I don't tell you I won't tell anyone. I just found out that Oldgods isn't my father. That my real father is my uncle Julian. I don't feel like going back there for a while. I was going to.

I meant to go back and cause a row, but sitting on the ferry I couldn't face it.'

He was watching me for signs of shock. He expected me to be as shocked as he had been. I thought about pretending that I hadn't known, but I caught my eye in the mirror, and there was a look of guilt in it.

'I knew,' I said.

'What?'

'I knew. Dervla told me last year. She knew because she was at university with your mother. She swore me to secrecy. I tried to bring the subject up a few times to see if you knew yourself, but I decided that either you didn't know or you didn't want to talk about it.'

'You knew?'

The tables were turned. But he made no effort to hide the reproach in his voice, and I wasn't capable of that all-dissolving smile. I tried to change the subject.

'What will you do next, if the Army's off?'

'I don't know. I'll think of something. What I need is to do one thing that I can live off for the rest of my life. Just one gadget, like the man who invented the cat's eyes in the road, and then live off the royalties. I don't want to work.'

I felt as though it was a child talking to me. I wanted to tell him to have some sense; that life wasn't like that. But I felt embarrassed to be the sensible, grown-up one. It was as if I had betrayed him by leaving him behind.

'Do you want a job?' I said.

'What?'

'I could do with some help on the farm. I only have Paddy Leary to help me, and he's getting on. Mikey Dwyer does the odd nixer for me, but getting work out of him is like getting blood from a turnip. You could work for me while you invent your gadget. Bed and board and wages. I don't know how much. Dervla handles all the money still. But it should be a bit.'

'I don't know,' he said. 'I'll think about it.'

We were pulling into the yard at Roscarmony.

He said, 'I don't know if I could see you as my employer. It could be the end of a beautiful friendship.'

I said, 'That's new. You were never given to clichés before. Listen. It'll be fine. The main reason I'm asking you is that I want to have you around. We'll have the house to ourselves for the winter. We could have the best time ever.'

He was smiling at me again, and with his smile I felt a great relief. 'All right,' he said. 'You're the boss.'

OCTOBER

He had been here a month. In a lot of ways it must have been one of the happiest months of my life. We worked during the day, and two or three nights a week we went drinking in Kilnure. Jean and Dervla came back at the weekends. Even when Dervla was there, Smallgods did all the cooking. He was a magician in the kitchen. Dervla said that he should start a restaurant, but he said that he wasn't prepared to work that hard.

In spite of his presence, I had begun to pine for Jean during the week. I told him that I thought I was in love with her. He laughed.

'Why are you laughing?'

'There isn't any such thing as love.'

'So what do you call it then?'

'Self-delusion,' he said.

For some reason, hearing that remark from him hurt me. I had come to think of our friendship in terms of some sort of love. Like the way I had loved my father, it was perfect, because it didn't need overt emotion or forced commitment. To hear Smallgods deny the existence of love was like hearing of a death. I hadn't yet told him about my madness in the summer. While he had been away I had been certain that he would understand. In his presence I wasn't so sure.

Next, I tried it out on Jean herself. It was in the middle of the night, after sex.

I said, 'I think I might be in love with you.'

'I know,' she said. Her voice was matter-of-fact.

'Well?'

'Well, what?'

'Well. I suppose, well nothing. If you think I'm in love with you too, then I must be. Are you in love with me?'

'Of course,' she said. 'Don't ask stupid questions and go to sleep.'

'Smallgods says there is no such thing as love.'

'Of course he does.'

'Why?'

'God,' she said. 'Why can't you ask these questions in the daytime? Smallgods is a lost soul. He is terrified.'

'Of love?'

'Of anything he can't control.'

'Do you think he's as fond of me as I am of him?'

'That isn't a good question. You are more vulnerable than he is. But I wouldn't worry about it. You aren't the same sort of people. You were once, but you aren't now.'

I was sitting up in the bed by now. 'So who has changed?'

'You haven't,' she said.

'I used to think that we'd be friends for the rest of our lives. I wish I could keep him here.'

'Don't be greedy,' she said.

She put her arm around my thigh, possessively. I realised for the first time that all of this had some bearing on her. That, at the very least, she had an interest in my emotional well-being. I thought about the love thing again. No one had ever told me that they loved me before. Not that she had said it outright.

'Say it outright,' I said.

'Say what?'

'That you love me.'

'Oh God,' she said. 'I love you. Now go to sleep.'

I suppose I was so unnerved by what Jean had said about Smallgods that I began to push him a bit too hard.

I would ask him questions like, 'Do you still believe in God?'

'What makes you think I ever did?'

'I used to hear you saying your prayers.'

He would flinch at a remark like that.

'I suppose so,' he said. 'I don't think about that sort of thing very much any more.' Then he would change the subject.

Things came to a head about the middle of October. We went out drinking on the Wednesday night and he met a girl he used to know. I could see that he didn't like her really; that it was only sex. By the end of the evening he had arranged to go home with her. Her parents were away. I drove back to Roscarmony on my own. For some reason I had trouble sleeping.

He didn't turn up for work in the morning, although he knew we were busy. I thought he might be having trouble getting a lift out from the town, so I found the girl's number in the book and phoned. When he came to the telephone he sounded sleepy and pleased with himself.

I said, 'I thought you might want a lift out.'

'Listen,' he said, 'I'm due a day off. I'll see you tonight.'

All that day the black depression that had haunted me in the summer was hovering near by. The only thing that kept it at bay was anger. Then he came back in the evening with his dissolving smile.

After supper, he was standing with his back to the Rayburn, leaning on the rail. I was at the table, sorting through feed bills so that they'd be ready for Dervla to deal with. I remember thinking, when I started to talk to him, that my motive was to punish him. For what, I don't know. On the other hand, the things I began to talk about had been stored up all the summer. The hovering depression that day had brought it all back to me.

He stood, and didn't answer anything I asked him or challenged him with. His expression was crucified and martyred, and that made me angry. I almost wanted to beat him with my fists because, by his silence, he was making me the villain. Whenever my voice rose, or I became pressing, he would look directly at me with a vacant accusation, and that look was so painful to me that I wanted to kill him.

'I lost my faith,' I said. 'There were times when I thought you were dead. I wept at your death. There were times when I wasn't weeping for you. When I knew my father was dying, I used to think: Well, at least I have Smallgods. I was convinced you would write to me before he died, and I would have an address, or better still, a phone number. I could call you the minute he died, and it wouldn't be so bad. But when he died there was nothing left. I was sure that the only reason you didn't contact me had to be that you were dead too. Before he died I thought you were immortal. After he died I couldn't see how you could possibly be alive.

'I remember sitting on a chair, and something bad and black came in the window at me, out of the night sky. I was so frightened that I fell off the chair. After that I stopped seeing that anything was possible. I couldn't believe that it was possible to breathe for another twenty-four hours. That was the day I wrote sixteen letters. But I didn't believe that you would ever get them. Because you were dead. I said things in those letters that I wouldn't have said to someone who was alive.

'I think, for a long time now, I have been in love with you. I know you say that love doesn't exist, but there isn't another word for it. I looked for another word and I kept coming back to the word love. It doesn't mean that I'm another Damon Mulrahey or anything like that. Sex is peripheral. It wasn't sex that made me fall in love with Jean. I could be wrong. I might be repressing something. But I believe that. What I mean by love is something too extraordinary to have anything to do with sex. But why should you believe me? It's as easy to tell a lie as it is to tell the truth.

'Right this minute; the way I'm talking, I feel as though I'm pestering you. The days seem to be gone when we used to walk around together with the sun shining out of our backsides. When we didn't have to do anything to be extraordinary. We just were. I think maybe you have changed.

'I missed you so much when you were in Australia, and because I thought you were dead I think I went mad. I tried to kill myself. In some ways, if all the people I loved were dead, that was the only way to see them again.

'On my birthday I got into the river. I was trying to walk along the bank as far as Ballynell, and the river got in my way, so I walked into it. It wasn't like suicide at all, it was just getting into the river and knowing that I would probably drown. Like all those fishermen in *David Copperfield*.

'The thing is, it was as though someone else wanted me to die, and I was obeying orders; being complicit because there was no good reason why I shouldn't. Anyway, I got caught on a salmon trap and I swam ashore again. That was where you came in.

'Do you remember when Orestes was born and you took the hippomane? I always believed that you had control of the destiny of that horse. The first creature I met when I came out of the river was Orestes, and I was convinced that it was you who had prevented me from drowning. After that I knew you were alive, and that you'd come back. Things got better.

'Most of the time I knew you were alive, but sometimes I thought you might be dead, and that you had become my guardian angel. In June I got bad again and decided to open a vein. Nothing could go wrong this time. I put on your black coat and went down to the marshes. But when I got there, the razor blades had fallen out of a hole in the pocket of your coat. Do you see? Each time it was you preventing me. I sat in the moonlight and laughed till I cried and cried till I laughed again.

'Things got better over the summer. Jean moved in. She kept me on the straight and narrow. I still had all the stuff about fear and death, but then I began to realise that death is only the end of fear. Fear of death is only fear's own survival instinct. I began to rationalise all the madness as something that was purely related to my father's death.

'But in between times, I had come to depend on you. And then you came back, and even though it seemed perfect, I know now that you have changed. What happened to you? You are more like other people, like other men, and less like Smallgods Temple.

'I am terrified that you are going to leave here, but this time, when you go away, it won't be like Jesus ascending into heaven. It will be like the leaving of an ordinary man who is afraid of life. And then when you are gone there won't be a guardian angel. There will be nothing to stop me, or nothing to stop death having me.

'Just tell me one thing. Are you afraid of me?'

The kitchen had darkened. The air smelled of linseed cake, burning in the bottom oven. The horses hadn't been fed.

'Will I turn the big light on?' I said.

'No.'

It was the first word he had spoken for over an hour.

I said, 'Have you ever been afraid? Have you ever had a fear that was so strong it was indescribable?'

'Yes.'

'There were days when I wanted to run from west to east to make the days shorter, so that even if I had to live a certain number of days, my life would still be shorter.'

'I know,' he said.

'Perhaps I did go mad. Do you think I am mad?'

'I don't know,' he said. 'You are very different. But there's no harm in that. I wouldn't like you if you weren't.'

When he said that, in exactly the same tone of voice as he had said it in Italy, I knew that everything was going to be fine. He came and sat on the other side of the table and held on to my hand. At least, I felt the pressure of a hand

and knew it must have been he because there was no one else in the room. I didn't dare to look at my hand, in case I was imagining it.

It was maybe ten years since I had cried in front of another man. During the nervous breakdown, I had always managed to pull myself together before anyone came into the room. That last time I had cried in public was when my pony broke his neck at the Lep of Adamstown. Most people were sympathetic, but a Forth and Bargy man on a big roan cob tried to get me to pull myself together by saying, 'Jesus, will you look at the big pussy babby.' At the time it made me angry, and I shouted at him to fuck off for himself. It was the first time I had ever sworn. More than anyone, I was angry with myself, because the embarrassment of being called a pussy babby seemed greater than my sorrow for the dead pony. I had always assumed that I loved that pony more than anything.

But Dervla said I was always dramatising myself.

Now, pussy babby or not, I could feel tears on my cheeks. Smallgods was staring at the table, and I hoped that he wouldn't look up and see them.

He said, 'John, whatever you do, or whatever I do, or whatever you think of me, don't die. Please.'

I had to make a sound that was like a gulp and he looked up.

'You big fool,' he said. 'If I ever catch you trying to commit suicide again, I'll kill you.'

That was the night he promised me our eternal friend-ship.

NOVEMBER

After the night in the kitchen things had seemed better for a day or two. I was congratulating myself that, by honesty and confrontation, I had saved a friendship. At the weekend he went to Dublin on his own, and when he came back he seemed closed off from me. He became less reliable on the farm; staying in bed late and taking a lot of days off. I couldn't bring myself to behave like a boss, so I said nothing. The night in the kitchen had been such an effort that I didn't have the energy to go through it again. And what would I say? I could only repeat myself. Because he had accused me of being a nagging wife, I was wary of that.

In November we went to Dublin for a party. It was the twenty-first birthday of a friend of Jean's, in a hotel near Stephen's Green. Everyone met in the International first, for a drink. Smallgods sat on one side of me, drinking gin and green chartreuse in equal parts. I was on Smithwick's. In the corner there was a youngish man with three shirts on, smoking a pipe and fiddling with a pearl ear-ring he wore while he talked to Jean about sex. Most of the men were in dinner jackets, and the girls wore a lot of costume jewellery and shingled haircuts. It looked a bit like the roaring twenties, come to Ireland sixty years too late. The pub was packed so tight that you couldn't stand up to give your seat to a girl even if you wanted to. It was a Thursday night, and Dublin was beginning to warm up for the weekend.

The man with three shirts and an ear-ring kept saying that he knew me from somewhere. I said that I didn't think so, and asked him what he did. He said that he was a writer; rewriting *The Epic of Gilgamesh*, set in a Ballymun high-rise with a heroin baron as the King of Erech. He gave the impression that he was on speed, but it could have been the way he talked.

Jean was sitting on my knee. I was beginning to be jealous of the way she was talking to the three shirts.

'I know you,' he said. 'I have you now. I had a great friend once who looked like you. But his hair fell out and he started a nightclub.'

'I know him,' Jean said. 'The fella who went around Limerick in yellow riding breeches. He was in graphics. What happened him?'

'His hair fell out and he started a nightclub.'

'You're not serious.'

'I am. My sister saw him last week.'

'John,' Smallgods said. 'Have you met Ciba Giegy?'

'No.'

'Show him, Assumpta.'

A drunk girl with a black band on her right arm pushed her hair back. There was a bloated goldfish set in resin hanging from her ear.

'She's very upset,' Smallgods said. 'He died this morning.'

The one with three shirts reached across and unhooked the goldfish from her ear, as if he wanted a closer look at it. Then he tilted his head back and put it in his mouth and swallowed it. Assumpta howled and there was a lot of drink spilled.

Jean said, 'Am I squashing you?'

And I said, 'No, this is heaven.'

We ended up sleeping on the floor of the writer with three shirts. Smallgods got up first and made us breakfast. On the bed, the writer and his girlfriend were eating toast and honey, and kissing with the honey still in their mouths. I thought they might be showing off, but I didn't like to say anything. Jean was asleep beside me, with both her legs wrapped around my left knee. Smallgods came and sat by my head while I drank milky tea. We could hear the sound of traffic, not far off, in Leeson Street.

Smallgods said, 'I have to go and see some people. I won't come back with you. I'll probably see you this evening.'

I said, 'We won't be going back yet. Probably not until the afternoon. Jean wants to see some exhibitions.'

'That's all right. I don't know how long I'll be. I'll get the bus down, or hitch or something.'

'So who are the people?' I said.

He looked at me hard for a second, as if he was warning me not to say anything. 'There's a chance of a job,' he said. 'It's something to do with films. I'm not sure.'

'Right. I'll see you tonight.' There was no point in objecting. I had no basis for an objection.

'Good luck,' I said, as he left the flat.

Later, I was waiting for Jean in Bewley's in Westmoreland Street. She had gone to an exhibition, while I had gone to Callaghan's for a new hat. I managed to get one of the high-backed seats, and sat in the clatter of coffee cups and the smell of puff pastry. There were twee old ladies from Ballsbridge and boys in leather jackets, at alternate tables. Then I saw someone I thought I recognised, sitting two tables away. She was wearing a lot of lipstick and her hair was piled up like an air hostess.

'Elsa?' I said.

'John G.? Holy Mother of God. What are you doing here? Is Godfrey with you? Isn't it amazing how you meet people in Dublin? I was only telling someone the other day about you, and here you are. What are you doing here?'

'I came up for a party. I'm waiting for Jean Spat. How are you?'

'Fine. Do you see anything of Godfrey these days?'

'He's staying with me at the moment. Down the country.'

'Oh,' she said.

'So what are you doing these days?'

'I'm working in Dublin,' she said. 'It's my day off.'

Then a baby in a pushchair, between her table and the next, dropped its soother. She reached down and picked the soother up and sucked it and put it back in the baby's mouth. Until that moment, I had assumed that the child belonged to the woman at the next table. I couldn't say anything. I knelt down in front of the child and studied it.

Eventually, I said, 'Is it a man or child? What's it called?'

'Patricia.'

'A girl. She looks like you. But she has his mouth. He never told me. Does he know?'

'He should,' she said. 'I've written him about fifty letters. I heard he went to Australia, but I wrote on the envelopes for them to be forwarded.' She looked at her watch. 'I have to go. You'll tell Godfrey you saw me?'

'I'm surprised you still want to speak to him.'

'So am I,' she said. 'But maybe I just want to give him a box in the mouth.'

I made her give me her address, and then she tottered away on her high-heels, manoeuvring the pushchair in front of her.

When he came back it was late, but I was still up. 'Well,' I said, 'did you get the job?'

'I think so. It isn't much. Mostly making the tea, from what I can gather. But it's a start. I always wanted to make films.'

'So you'll be moving to Dublin?'

'I suppose so. What's the matter?'

I didn't know how to phrase it. I didn't want to accuse him. It was possible that he hadn't received any of Elsa's letters. I had spent most of the day trying to make a case for his innocence.

'I was in Bewley's. I saw Elsa, and Patricia.'

That was clever of me, though unintentionally so. If he didn't recognise the name Patricia, then everything was all right.

But he said, 'What did she look like? I often thought it would be nice to see her.'

So I exploded. 'How can you say that? You're a liar. And a complete bastard.'

He hunched his body, like a dog who was expecting a beating.

'I know,' he said.

'Sweet Jesus. It isn't human.'

'So,' he said. 'I'm not human. Why do you bother talking to me? What if I don't want to spend my entire life rushing about, loving people and being responsible? You won't be able to make me live by your values.'

'That isn't what I meant.'

'Oh, forget it,' he said.

'No. I can't. At least now you are talking to me; saying something.'

'No I'm not. Why should I talk, or say the things you want?'

'Because that isn't you. Something has changed you, and you're afraid to go back. You're afraid of everything. You always have been, but before you didn't let your fear control you.'

'What's it got to do with you?'

'I thought you were dead once, and I nearly died because of it. And what I can see in front of me now is a dead person.'

I talked on at him. It must have been for nearly an hour, and as I talked his body seemed to collapse, until he was hunched again at the edge of a chair, and then, I don't know what happened.

In the middle of one of my sentences, he went off like a bomb. He screamed, and sustained the scream, and crashed about the kitchen, breaking everything his hands and feet and head touched, and then he collapsed on to the floor, banging his head and fists against the tiles. At first, I stood and watched as if I was made of stone, but then I realised he was going to hurt himself and I got him in a half-Nelson until he was quiet. He was sobbing, not like a child but more like an animal, between my two arms, both of us kneeling on the floor.

Jean had heard the noise and come downstairs. She stood naked in the doorway. He saw her.

'I'm all right,' he said to her. 'I'm all right. I'm sorry. Go back to bed.'

She looked at me, and the battered kitchen, and the blood on Smallgods' hands and face. She opened her mouth to say something, but Smallgods said he was all right again, and I nodded at her. 'It's all right,' I said. And she turned and went away.

DECEMBER

Jean sat across Clytemnestra with the reins dropped to the buckle. In a bowler hat, with her hair in a net, she looked like someone else. An odd hound appeared in the hedge, and disappeared back again. The day was balmy and there was no scent. People were shouting either 'Ware Hound!' or 'Mind the fucking dogs, Moore', depending on their social pretensions. Oedipus was acting the maggot that day, snorting and skipping around the lane like a three year old. Clytemnestra behaved impeccably for Jean. There wasn't a flicker out of either of them.

Smallgods had only lasted two weeks in his job with the film company. Before he had gone up, he had promised me that he would go and see Elsa and the baby. I found out later that he hadn't. When he had returned to Wexford, it was Ballynell he had gone to, not Roscarmony. He had discovered, apparently, that there can be worse things than living with your family. I wouldn't have known he was back, if Dervla hadn't told me. Dervla asked me if I had fallen out with him.

I said, 'No. What makes you think that?'

'Nothing,' she said, and she covered me with a look of disbelief. Dervla seemed happy these days. She did less housework at the weekends, and spent her time studying and writing. She would come drinking in Kilnure with Jean and me. Bit by bit, she was shedding all her auntieness.

The day's hunting wore on, and there was hardly a scamper. There was already a bit of snow over the Blackstairs, and when the afternoon came a great chill came with it. Hounds went home, and we had a four-mile hack back to the box. The cold made trotting uncomfortable, so we walked the horses.

'You still haven't seen Smallgods?' Jean asked.

'No. Not lately.'

Small bits of wet snow began to land on the horses' manes. The cold buried itself in our feet.

'So what happened?' she said.

'I think I've lost him.'

'Don't dramatise yourself,' she said. 'What happened?'

'He said that I had to give him some time, and when he was able to deal with me again he would come and see me. I think I was too intense. He was afraid of me. I don't know. You probably know as much about it as I do. It was a bit like a horrible story Dervla used to tell me to scare me to sleep when I was little. About a man and a bear. They both lived in the woods and one day the man found the bear with a thorn in his paw and took the thorn out, and they were friends after that and all the rest of it. They used to go hunting together, and the bear became very fond of the man. One year, the winter was so bad that there was no game to be had, and the bear and the man got very thin. I know the bear should have been hibernating, but when we said that to Dervla she said that it was too cold that winter to sleep. Anyway, the two of them were stomping home through the wood, with nothing in their game bag, and the man blew on his nails to warm them.

'"What are you doing?" the bear said.

'"Blowing on my nails to warm them."

'"Well, I never," the bear said.

'They went back to the man's hut for a cup of tea, which they had to drink black, because it was so cold that the cow had frozen to death. So the tea was very hot, and the man blew over his cup to cool it.

'"What are you doing?" said the bear.

' "I'm blowing my tea to cool it."

' "Well, I never,' said the bear, whose stomach was rumbling with the hunger. "You claim to warm something and cool something with the same breath. You must be a liar."

'And before the man could answer, the bear ate him.'

'I don't get it,' Jean said.

'Neither do I. I was hoping that you would. If you don't get it, no one can.'

The snow came driving at us. We had our collars up, and our chins dug into them, and the horses walked with their heads turned into the snow, their muzzles nearly touching our boots.

Dervla was waiting for us at the boxes. She had driven us over in the morning, and then unhitched the Landrover to go shopping in Wexford.

'I don't know what kept you,' she said. 'I was getting worried. Mary Howlin came past me half an hour ago. I have a terrible feeling.'

We had to drive slowly in the blizzard. It took an hour and a half to get to Roscarmony.

'Did you remember to get Stasia Dwyer's biscuits?' I said.

'I did.'

By the time we had dried and fed the horses, it was long after dark. I went into the kitchen last. Dervla and Jean had piled all the shopping on the kitchen table and were sorting it out and putting it away. I sat on the chair by the door to pull off my spurs. Just by my right shoulder there was a dent in the wall, where Smallgods' fist had hit it the night he went mad. As I pulled on the straps of the spurs, I was thinking about the Christmas morning when I had emptied them from the stocking on to Gerard's bed. Out of the corner of my eye I saw an unfamiliar coat lying on the floor in the porch.

Dervla said, 'Shut that door, John. It's freezing.'

'Just a minute,' I said.

As I picked the coat up, something fell from the pocket. I brought it, and the coat, into the kitchen. It was Gerard's passport.

'Gerard must be home,' I said.

I went rushing up the stairs to find my brother, with Dervla shouting after me that I should have taken my boots off first. There was a light on in his room, but I thought at first that he wasn't there. Then, beneath the nihilistic posters that still hung on his wall, I saw him slumped in the corner by the bed. He had a belt, or a strap or something, tied around his arm, and a syringe in his other hand. His tongue was sticking out and his eyes were open. He looked ill. It wasn't until I put my hand on his shoulder that I realised he was dead.

CHRISTMAS

When I spoke to Mrs Temple afterwards she said that she had been watching him from the window. Smallgods had gone out to get the post and had a brief conversation with the postman. He watched the postman drive away, and when the van had gone he dropped the mail from his hand on to the ridges of frozen mud that covered the yard. She went out to see what the matter was, but by the time she reached the back door he had crossed the yard and was walking down the field towards the river. She called after him to take a coat, but he didn't hear. He was walking fast like an automaton.

It seems that there had been a misunderstanding. The postman had told him the Young Moore was dead of an overdose, and Smallgods had assumed that Young Moore was me, and that an overdose was the same thing as a suicide. He must have been in a bit of a turmoil walking down and across the fields, thinking that I was dead and that he was responsible for it. Mrs Temple said that it was two hours before he came back to the house. His hands were blue and his fingernails mauve. He told her that I was dead and then he went about muttering to himself; cursing me for not waiting for him; for not staying alive until he was ready to deal with me. He packed a small bag and left the house, not saying where he was going.

Mrs Temple phoned Dervla with her sympathies, and after the two of them had spoken at cross purposes for a few minutes, the matter was set straight, but not in time. I drove to Ballynell as fast as I could, and drove to Rosslare afterwards, hoping to find Smallgods hitch-hiking on the roads. Near Killanick I realised that my intention was not only to tell Smallgods that I was alive, but that it was Gerard who was dead; as though my brother's death could be good news. That was when I gave up the hunt and came home.

Smallgods had gone for good. The readiness with which he had accepted my death only struck me as extraordinary a long time afterwards. I sometimes hear about him from mutual friends of his and Jean's, but it is up to him to contact me, if such a contact is ever likely to happen. He must know by now that I am the one who is living.

FRANK RONAN
A PICNIC IN EDEN

Does the world allow for true love between a man and a woman? And if not, can one call the friendship between two men love? Adam Parnell, an expatriate Irishman, and Dougie Millar, a taciturn Scot, are in different ways looking for a return to innocence, living with their wives amid the beauties of the Western Isles. Both men find in each other the means to confront their childhoods – and the demons that drove one of their fathers to drink, the other to suicide – and to discover whether, once left behind, there can be any return to Eden.

'An extraordinarily fine writer . . . his novel is a shifting tableau of brilliances and oddities . . . The precise lyrical beauty of the prose – poetic but never purple – is a vehicle for a disturbingly dark vision, for gut-punching philosophies and flashes of wit'
Elle

'A rich and assured look at the ways parents can sour a child's capacity for adult love . . . Ronan has an impressive wisdom and breadth of vision'
Cosmopolitan

'An absorbing novel . . . Ronan is a relentlessly honest, quirky and exciting new writer'
The Daily Mail

'Crisp and elegantly written'
The Observer

'Makes one impatient to see what this talented writer will do next'
Times Literary Supplement

'Ronan writes in an easy, limpid style; he has fluency and a light touch'
Independent on Sunday

'A PICNIC IN EDEN continues in the same rich literary vein he tapped so successfully with THE MEN WHO LOVED EVELYN COTTON'
The Times

'Both refreshing and often disturbing'
The Irish Press

sceptre

WILLIAM RIVIERE

A VENETIAN
THEORY OF HEAVEN

This moving and elegiac novel charts the sentimental education of Francesca Ziani, a young, naïve student who lodges with her cousin Amedea in a crumbling Venetian *palazzo*. Rich, reckless and unashamedly patrician, Amedea feels trapped by the stagnant society in which she moves and, contemptuous of the effects on her English husband and their small son, makes a dramatic attempt to break free.

'A marvellous book . . . subtle and gripping . . . Enthrals and disturbs in the deceptively leisurely manner of Henry James's Venetian idyll THE ASPERN PAPERS'
John Bayley in the Evening Standard

'A hymn to beauty . . . The real hero is the city itself, with its dark, thick waters and decaying beauties'
Nicci Gerrard in The Observer

'He writes with authority. He writes beautifully too . . . He dares to treat love, and the death of love, as seriously as lovers treat it . . . I look forward with eagerness and impatience to what he does next'
Allan Massie in The Scotsman

'A beautifully written and captivating tragedy'
Laura Connelly in Time Out

'An interesting and intelligent novelist'
John Melmoth in The Sunday Times

'Written beautifully, tenderly, its passion a velvet blackness . . . he encircles the dying of one love affair and the flaring of another with amazing chameleon stealth and imagination'
Tom Adair in Scotland on Sunday

'Exotic, unforgettable characters people these pages . . . Compellingly told, exquisitely drawn'
Irish Sunday Independent

sceptre

D. M. THOMAS
FLYING IN TO LOVE

John F. Kennedy's death in 1963 ended the hopes and dreams of a multitude, yet he continues to haunt the world's imagination. And it is with the shifting perspectives of a dream that this riveting novel explores Kennedy's character, his assassination and its enduring legacy, memorably recreating this most magnetic of men in all his flawed splendour.

'The sense of intimacy and immediacy the author cooks up is as thrilling as it is poignant'
The Times

'His most absorbing fiction for years . . . Thomas cleverly twists the tale into a myth of his own making . . . his juggling with past, present and possibility has the knack of magic . . . a brilliant gloss on the piece of history we all shared'
The Mail on Sunday

'Ingenious, almost audacious, in his approach to history . . . we witness Thomas at his most moving and complex'
The Sunday Times

'An unusual, imaginative novel, cunningly constructed and written with an almost populist assurance'
The Daily Telegraph

'The principals step onto the bright Dallas stage as if for the first time. There is a sense of excitement one would not have thought possible in the telling of such an old tale . . . it succeeds brilliantly in illuminating the no man's land of pain between sleeping and waking'
The Sunday Telegraph

sceptre

NIGEL WATTS

WE ALL LIVE IN A HOUSE CALLED INNOCENCE

James is turning thirty, stuck in the dismal routine of a librarian's job and a long-term relationship with his girlfriend. Then a human hand-grenade explodes into his life in the shape of Tad, a gay wheelchair-bound writer of pornographic stories. Before James knows it, he has an outrageously uninhibited new friend who goads him to take a fresh look at life, dispense with guilt and put his sexual fantasies into practice. For James, it's the first dangerous step on a journey into himself that could lead anywhere.

'The most moving, tender and funny exposé of a sexist creep I've ever read . . . a LUCKY JIM for the '90s'
Time Out

'Funny and wonderfully honest, it's totally riveting'
Company

'Utterly likeable . . . James Morrison's interior life is portrayed with uncanny skill, a melange of sexual speculation and frantic observation of the world around him'
The Times

'A right shocker and a real corker for the Nineties . . . Watts clearly has the ability to play a variety of roles with outlandish elegance'
Daily Mail

'Watts has psychologically stunning insights and empathy . . . wise and moving'
The Sunday Times

'Gives a rare insight into male insecurity'
Today

sceptre